OB
am

NOV - 2005

The
Midnight
Before
Christmas

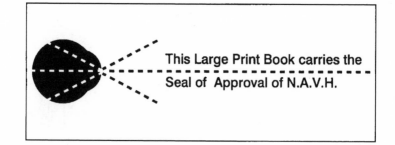

This Large Print Book carries the
Seal of Approval of N.A.V.H.

The Midnight Before Christmas

William Bernhardt

Thorndike Press • Waterville, Maine

Published in 2005 by arrangement with The Ballantine Publishing Group, a division of Random House, Inc.

Thorndike Press® Large Print Famous Authors.

The tree indicium is a trademark of Thorndike Press.

The text of this Large Print edition is unabridged.
Other aspects of the book may vary from the original edition.

Set in 16 pt. Plantin by Elena Picard.

Printed in the United States on permanent paper.

Library of Congress Cataloging-in-Publication Data

Bernhardt, William, 1960–
    The midnight before Christmas / by William Bernhardt.
      p. cm. — (Thorndike Press large print famous authors)
    ISBN 0-7862-7877-3 (lg. print : hc : alk. paper)
    1. Women lawyers — Fiction. 2. Large type books.
I. Title. II. Thorndike Press large print famous authors series.
PS3552.E73147M5 2005
  813′.54—dc22
                                      2005014263

For all our friends at St. Dunstan's

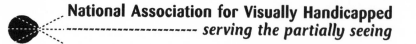

National Association for Visually Handicapped
serving the partially seeing

As the Founder/CEO of NAVH, the only national health agency solely devoted to those who, although not totally blind, have an eye disease which could lead to serious visual impairment, I am pleased to recognize Thorndike Press★ as one of the leading publishers in the large print field.

Founded in 1954 in San Francisco to prepare large print textbooks for partially seeing children, NAVH became the pioneer and standard setting agency in the preparation of large type.

Today, those publishers who meet our standards carry the prestigious "Seal of Approval" indicating high quality large print. We are delighted that Thorndike Press is one of the publishers whose titles meet these standards. We are also pleased to recognize the significant contribution Thorndike Press is making in this important and growing field.

Lorraine H. Marchi, L.H.D.
Founder/CEO
NAVH

★ Thorndike Press encompasses the following imprints: Thorndike, Wheeler, Walker and Large Print Press.

"I would rather live in a world where my life is surrounded by mystery than live in a world so small that my mind could comprehend it."
— *Harry Emerson Fosdick*

1

He just couldn't stand it anymore. He cocked his arm back, clenched his fist, and propelled it on a line drive toward the other man's jaw.

His fist connected with a sickening thud. The other man's body crumpled to the front lawn like a hand puppet without a hand.

Bonnie screamed. "Frank! *Frank!*" She pressed her hands against her cheeks, seemingly paralyzed with shock and fear. "Carl, what have you done?"

She crouched beside the stricken man, cradling his head in her lap, brushing her hand over his closed eyes. "Frankie, are you all right? Speak to me! *Please!*"

Carl stepped back, somewhat subdued now that his opponent was out of commission. "I didn't think I hit him that hard."

"You maniac!" Bonnie shouted. "He's unconscious!"

Carl inched forward. "Let me take a look at him."

"Get back! Stay away! Help! *Help!*"

Neighbors began to emerge from the Federal-style homes lining the streets. Women in aprons stood in elaborate fan doorways, men burdened with packages huddled beneath porticos, all of them wondering what the commotion was about. A crowd gathered at the closest corner.

Carl grabbed Bonnie by the arms and jerked her to her feet. "Stop yelling! *Stop!*" He raised his hand as if to slap her.

"Help me!" Bonnie continued. "Someone *please* help me!"

Out the corner of his eye, Carl could see some of the neighbors cautiously moving forward. One woman was dialing a cellular phone.

He lowered his hand. "I just want to see my son!"

"You can't. He's mine!"

"He's ours, Bonnie."

"The judge gave him to me."

"The judge gave you custody —"

"And he gave you nothing!"

"Bonnie, please. I have to see Tommy. I *need* to see him."

"Why? So you can beat him up, too? I'm not letting you anywhere near him!"

Carl clenched his teeth. "I have to see him, Bonnie. He's my son!"

"Over my dead body!"

Carl's face became grim. "Don't say that, Bonnie. Don't say that."

Frank, the man sprawled across the front lawn, stirred. He propped himself up on one arm, blinking rapidly.

"Frankie!" Bonnie ran to his side. "Are you all right?"

Frank rubbed his jaw. "I . . . think I'll live. But there's an off-key symphony playing in my head."

"Frankie, go into the house."

"I'm not going to leave you here with —"

"Frankie, please. It's for the best."

Frank hesitated, as if itching to disagree, but finally relented. With some effort, he pulled himself to his feet and hobbled toward the front door of the house.

Bonnie whirled back on Carl. "You could've killed him!"

"I wish." Carl pounded his fists together. "That sorry SOB sees more of my boy than I do."

"That's because Frank doesn't lose his temper." She drew in her breath. "And he doesn't drink."

Carl's face seemed to dissolve. "Bonnie . . ." He stretched out his hand.

11

"I've been going to meetings."

"Save it for your parole officer, Carl. I can smell your breath from here."

"Bonnie, please —"

"I don't want you hanging around, Carl. I don't want you stalking us, harassing us. And I especially don't want you anywhere near Tommy."

"But, Bonnie, it's Christmas Eve!"

"I don't care, Carl. I can't trust you. I can't take the risk."

"But it's Christmas Eve! A family should be together."

"The family *is* together, Carl. Me, Tommy, and Frank."

"*I'm* his father. Not —"

"You don't know what being a father means, Carl. You never did."

"Bonnie, I'm begging you —"

"It's time you learned that no means no, Carl." A few of the braver neighbors were edging closer, crossing the street. "I can't take this anymore. I can't take being scared all the time, worrying that you're going to do some permanent damage. I want you to go away and never come back."

"Bonnie!"

"You heard me, Carl. *Go away!*"

His fists tightened like tiny balls of super-concentrated energy. Rage boiled through his body, coursed through his veins. "I can't accept that, Bonnie. I won't."

"You don't have any choice." She ran through the front door of the house and slammed it between them.

"No!" Carl rushed forward, his face flushed with anger. He pounded on the front door, beating it so hard it splintered the wood. "Let me in! Let me *in!*"

One of the neighbor men ran forward, grabbing Carl around the shoulders, trying to pull him back. "C'mon now, Carl. Let's calm down."

Carl whirled around and shoved the neighbor against the chest. The man stumbled backward, tripping on the front steps. He tumbled down, cracking his head against the concrete sidewalk.

"I want in!" Carl roared. "Do you hear me, Bonnie? I want in!"

"Go away!" she shrieked from the other side of the door. "The police are on their way!"

"I *will* see my boy!" He pounded the front door again and again and again, sending paint chips flying in all directions, making the whole frame of the house shudder. He was making a dent, but even in his rage, he knew he would never get in this way.

He jumped over the hedge and azaleas and crossed to the front window just to the left of the door. "I want in, Bonnie!" he howled.

"No!"

Carl reared back his fist and sent it sailing through the window. Glass shattered all around him as his fist broke through to the other side. The harsh insistent beep of the security alarm began to pulse. Blood dripped across his arm and down the windowpane.

Carl cried out in pain. His hand was sliced in more places than he knew, and it hurt. But he didn't let that stop him. He twisted his fingers around and reached up to unfasten the window lock.

Bonnie appeared on the other side of the window. "Stop it, Carl! Stop it!"

"All I want is to see my boy."

"I can't let you do that, Carl. I can't take the risk."

"I'm coming in. And you can't stop me." His fingers touched the window lock.

"No," Bonnie whispered. She grabbed his protruding hand.

"Leave me alone!" Carl bellowed.

"I can't." She took his fist in both of her hands and jerked his arm upward, impaling it on a jagged piece of broken window glass.

Pain coursed through Carl's arm, then his body, like the ripple of sheet lightning. He screamed, then jerked his hand back through the window, clutching it close against his chest. Blood gushed from the open wound.

His face was spotted with blood and sweat. "You can't stop me," he said, gasping. "No matter what."

"He isn't here," Bonnie said, tears spilling from her eyes. "Tommy isn't even here. Please go away."

The sound of a police siren cut through the morning air. It was still several blocks away, but moving closer at top speed.

Carl pressed his wounded arm against his mouth. He clamped his other hand down on it, trying to stanch the flow of blood. "This isn't over," he said, gazing at his ex-wife through the spiderwebbed windowpane. "I'll be back."

He turned and raced down the street, barreling through a chain of spectators, ducking into the backyard three houses down.

Even after he had disappeared from sight, Bonnie's breathing didn't slow down. Her heartbeat didn't settle, and she couldn't stop clutching herself. Because she knew what he had said was true. She knew this wasn't over.

She knew he would be back.

2

Megan McGee readjusted the rearview mirror so she could get a better look at her beard. It wasn't easy. There was barely enough room inside her tiny two-door Toyota for herself, much less an English bulldog. There was absolutely no room for primping. Still, she wanted to look her best when she knocked on the door, although why it mattered to her she couldn't imagine. Certainly no one back at the law firm cared. No one at Santa's Helpers was watching. And God — well, best not to get her started on that subject.

The English bulldog squatting in the passenger seat, Jasper, made a grunting, spitting noise. A stream of gas emitted from his hindquarters while a sheepish expression crossed his squashed English face. He stretched forward, rubbing his very wet nose against Megan's hand. A pool of drool spilled out of his mouth and dripped down her arm.

For the record, Megan reminded herself, I hate this dog.

Perhaps hate was too strong a word. Perhaps it was sufficient to say she didn't particularly much care for the beast. She had never wanted the dog, never wanted any dog. She had inherited him from a neighbor who was moving to Hawaii, where the quarantine laws were quite strict. They couldn't bear the thought of poor Jasper being cooped up in a cage for a year or more, they had said, so would Megan please please *please* take care of him for them?

Just imagine. They go off to Hawaii while she's stuck in Oklahoma City with the Hound of the Baskervilles. It wasn't enough that he was the worst, most plug-ugly creature she had ever seen in her life. He was also a finicky eater, and usually dripped and dragged his food all over her apartment. What's more, he needed digestion medicine two times a day, which required her to open his slime-lined mouth to deliver the goods. And that wasn't even mentioning — this was the topper — doggie suppositories. Every day without fail.

She had thought about taking him to the

pound or putting him to sleep, but she just couldn't bring herself to do it. So here she was, tootling around town on Christmas Eve, with the Pet from Hell.

What a life she led.

Megan gazed up at the steely gray sky. Last night's predictions of snow might still come true, she realized. Which would be good for those trying to get into the Christmas spirit, although bad for those — like Megan — who still had driving to do.

She slid out of the car and tried to smooth the pronounced wrinkles in her borrowed suit. Red faux fur with white lining. A red-and-white stocking cap. And of course, the full white beard. Wasn't she just the cutest Santa that ever was?

Probably not, Megan thought, sighing. When she'd picked up the suit at Santa's Helpers, she had noticed a new associate from Crowe Dunlevy who definitely outstripped her in the cute department. What did she expect, for Pete's sake? She was thirty-seven and not getting any younger or prettier. Especially not with a bushy white beard on her chin.

Oh, please, she told herself, don't get started on that again. You have a job to do. And an important one at that. Cookie deliveries. Meals on Wheels, the Christmas edition. Ho, ho, ho, and here's a little something sweet to get you through the night. That was her mission. Bringing a little sunshine into the lives of the poor, the elderly, the lonely.

Jeepers, she thought. She should be making a delivery to herself.

She carefully removed her blue plate from the backseat and took it out of the protective bubble wrap. She loved this plate. She'd bought it in England several years before, when she had been in Canterbury for the St. Dunstan millennial birthday celebration. It was nineteenth-century Spode, with a blue-etched scene of bucolic British country life. It had cost her a small fortune, but she loved it dearly. One of the best things about these cookie deliveries, as far as she was concerned, was that she got a chance to show off her plate.

She grabbed the giant bag of cookies, poured some onto the plate, arranged them as artfully as she could manage, and headed for the door, trying not to trip. As she had learned at her last several stops, her agility was considerably hampered by having her feet encased in shiny black boots about three sizes too big.

She rang the doorbell and waited. She heard some shuffling on the other side of the door, but she had learned not to get impatient. According to the fact sheet, the woman inside, one Teresa Tucker, was eighty-four years old, living alone and managing quite fine, thank you. Let her take as long as she wanted.

At last the door creaked open, and a wizened face appeared in the opening. "Yes?"

"Ho, ho, ho!" Megan said, in the deepest voice she could muster. "Merry Christmas!"

"I've already given," the woman replied. She began to close the door.

"Wait just a minute, Mrs. Tucker." Megan planted a brick-size boot in the doorway. "You can't shut the door on ol' Santa."

"I may be old," Mrs. Tucker said, "but I'm not senile or blind. You're not Santa. You're a woman."

Megan coughed. "Well then, I'm Mrs. Santa."

"I don't normally think of Mrs. Santa as sporting a beard," Mrs. Tucker answered. "But I suppose anything could happen that far north."

Somehow Megan didn't think Mrs. Tucker was quite into the spirit of the thing.

"I've got something for you," Megan

said, abandoning the basso profundo voice. She brought the cookie-filled plate around to view.

"Oh, joy," Mrs. Tucker said wearily. "What is it this year?"

"Cookies! Ho, ho, ho!"

"Cookies? Why, I haven't been able to eat cookies since —" She stopped in mid-sentence. All at once her eyes glowed like Christmas lights. "Oh, but I do like this!" She snatched the bundle out of Megan's hands, plate and all.

"Wait," Megan said hesitantly, "I think you've got the —"

"I do *love* blue china." Mrs. Tucker dumped the cookies into a nearby bowl and clutched the plate against her bosom. "When I was younger and Herbert was still alive, we used to travel all across Europe, visiting flea markets and resale shops. He would hunt for those insipid Hummel figurines, and I would collect all the blue china I saw." Her eyes drifted upward dreamily. " 'Course I had to sell it after Herbert died and the taxes had to be paid and things got bad. Never thought I'd have any again." She looked at Megan and beamed. "Till you showed up at my door."

Megan coughed. "Um, ma'am, I think you misunderstand —"

"I tried to be brave when I had to sell it all off. Tried not to think about it afterward. But I couldn't help myself. I do miss those beautiful plates. Miss them every livelong day."

"Mrs. Tucker, I'm sorry, but the plate isn't —"

"I can't tell you how much this means to me, child. I'll cherish this plate for the rest of my days."

"Mrs. Tucker! I'm trying to tell you that —" Megan stopped cold. She peered into the woman's eyes, those dark eyes that now, for the first time in who knows how long, seemed bright and alive.

Mrs. Tucker's hands began to tremble slightly. She loosened her grip on the plate. "You . . . were saying something?"

Megan took a deep breath, closed her eyes, then nodded. "Merry Christmas, Mrs. Tucker."

"Oh. *Oh!*" A radiant smile erased the wrinkles of her face. "Thank you. Thank you very much." She winked. "Santa."

Megan boot-flopped her way back to her car. Well, what's a plate, anyway? she told herself. Eight years of being a priest, she never once put a smile on anyone's face like that one.

She had almost reached the car door

when she heard the cry from behind. "Wait! Saaaanta!"

Mrs. Tucker was hobbling down the sidewalk after her, carrying what looked like a large framed picture of some sort.

Mrs. Tucker finally caught up to Megan, then stopped to catch her breath. "You've been so kind. I wanted you to have something."

"That's not necessary, ma'am."

"No, I insist. Even if you don't want it for yourself, maybe you can pass it along to someone else. It's a lovely piece of artwork. Very valuable."

Artwork? Megan's eyebrows rose. What a coup if she could bring a valuable piece of art back to the Legal Services offices. They could sell it at their annual auction. Something like that might pay their operational bills for a year.

"I'll miss it," Mrs. Tucker continued, "but who knows? Maybe this could mean as much to someone else as that plate means to me."

"Could I see it?" Megan asked.

"Of course." Mrs. Tucker turned it around. The framed material was not canvas but lush black velvet. Megan's eyes fairly bulged as she gazed upon the subject — or, more accurately, subjects:

several bulldogs huddled around a poker table.

"Isn't it lovely?" Mrs. Tucker said. "My late Herbert just adored it."

"Did he?" Megan said evenly. "Herbert must've been an interesting man."

"Not really. But he did love his bull-dogs." She pressed the picture into Megan's hands. "Here."

"Oh, gosh. I don't know —"

"I insist." She started back toward the house. "And thank you again. I have to de-cide where I'm going to hang my new plate!"

Megan nodded and waved. "Merry Christmas!" She turned, opened the car door, and tossed the alleged artwork into the backseat. "Jasper, meet your new bulldog buddies!"

Jasper grinned, and a huge pool of doggie spittle dripped down onto the pas-senger seat.

"Way to go, Rudolph." She slid into the driver's seat and turned the ignition. "To the top of the porch, to the top of the wall, now dash away, dash away, dash away all!"

3

"Just leave the bottle."

"Carl, I will not leave the bottle."

"I said leave it."

"And I said *no!*"

Carl and the bartender hunched over the single-chair table and glared at each other, their eyes searing the void between them.

Carl Cantrell clenched the top of the whiskey bottle, his hand wrapped around the bartender's. "I need a drink," he said, slurring his words more than a bit.

"You've had a drink. You've had several drinks. And the day's barely begun."

Carl yanked harder, trying to get control of the bottle, but the bartender stubbornly refused. Their arms worked back and forth like pistons.

Joe the bartender stopped pulling, reached around with his other hand, and extended Carl's arm. He saw the strip of torn shirt wrapped around his forearm, now stained with blood. "Jiminy Christmas, Carl. What've you done to yourself?"

Carl jerked his arm back. "It's nothin'. Just a scratch."

"A scratch? What's wrong with you?"

"Nothing's wrong with me. 'Cept I need a drink."

"Forget it."

Carl grabbed the bottle again. "I need a little somethin' in the mornings. Just to get my heart started."

"You keep drinking like this, your heart's gonna stop dead in its tracks." The bartender jerked the bottle free. "One more drink, Carl. That's it."

Carl made a hiccuping noise. "Then make it a double. I'm in pain here."

"One more drink." The bartender pulled Carl's shot glass closer and poured. "And after that, I want you out of here. And I don't want to see you around anymore. Got it?"

Carl's watery eyes widened. "Whadd're you saying, Joe?"

"You know what I'm saying. I don't want you around no more. You don't belong here."

"Joe . . ." A lump seemed to catch in his throat. "I been comin' here forever. Me and the boys —"

"You ain't been with the boys for years and you damn well know it. Those days are done. You tossed 'em away with about ten tons of hooch."

"But, Joe . . ." He reached out with his good arm and was embarrassed to see that it trembled. "This is my place."

"This is a cop bar," Joe replied, turning away. "And you ain't been a cop for a good long time."

Carl watched as Joe faded into the dark recesses of the bar. His head hung in place, seemingly frozen, as if he didn't have the strength to move it. He felt tired and washed out.

His eyes had the misfortune to light upon the wall-length mirror behind the bar. He could see himself, draped over this rickety, unbalanced table like a human vulture. His face was drawn and his hair was a mess; he looked pathetic. His chin was dark with stubble. Come to think of it, he hadn't shaved this morning, had he? Maybe not the day before, either. Maybe not since he lost the job at the hardware store — his fifth in a year.

Jeez. He pounded himself on the forehead. No wonder Bonnie wouldn't see him, wouldn't let him see his boy. He looked like death warmed over. If he'd bumped into himself on the street, he probably wouldn't let Tommy talk to him, either. Just a bum, his son would think. Some worn-out, washed-up rummy. Keep your kids away. Don't let them be infected by the thick smell of flop sweat. Don't let them be contaminated by the man who reeks of failure.

He picked up the shot glass and downed it. The liquor burned his throat, coating his stomach with a new layer of confidence and self-respect. The sudden warmth surged through his arms, his legs, his head.

He felt better. But how long would it last?

One thing was certain — he wasn't welcome at Joe's anymore. Where else could he go? There weren't many places open this time of the morning, and on Christmas Eve, no less. Most people weren't bar-hopping on the twenty-fourth of December. Even most rummies had someplace else to go. Even the most pathetic drunks usually had a family.

But not Carl. Not anymore.

I'm all alone, he thought. The words were a relentless pounding inside his brain. I'm all alone.

He banged the empty shot glass down on the table, making it rock back and forth on its not-on-the-level legs. It wasn't right. Not right at all. Sure, he'd been going through a rough patch. Times were hard. But that was no reason for Bonnie to bail out. That was no reason to take away his son, his Tommy, the only thing that still mattered in his life.

He pulled his wallet out of his back pocket and removed a creased and slightly torn photo. Tommy and him, three Christmases ago. They were standing in front of the tree, Tommy in his jammies going ape over the Dinosaur Mountain play set Santa had brought him. Carl sitting just beside him, grinning from ear to ear like the proud daddy he was.

Three Christmases ago. And in three short years, the whole damn world had changed. Tommy didn't even look like this now.

Carl picked up the shot glass and hurled it across the room. It smashed into the wall on the opposite side, leaving a dark, dripping stain on the fading wallpaper.

Joe hustled out of the shadows. "I want you gone, Carl! Now!"

"I'm goin', I'm goin'."

"I'll give you thirty seconds. Then I'm calling the cops."

"The cops?"

"Yeah, the cops. You remember them,

don't you, Carl? The boys in blue. That nice shiny uniform you used to wear? Well, they're gonna be in here to haul your butt to the pokey if you're still around in thirty seconds!" He checked his watch. "Make that twenty."

"I'm gone," Carl muttered. "Thanks for everything."

He shoved the photo back in his wallet, threw some money on the table, grabbed his jacket, and headed for the door. His arm twinged as he twisted it back into the coat sleeve, but the whiskey had deadened the pain just enough to make it bearable.

He stepped onto the sidewalk and was nearly bowled over by shoppers rushing both ways at once. Everyone seemed to be in a hurry. Of course they were, Carl thought. Everyone has places to go, people to be with. Everyone but me.

He spotted a group of carolers on the opposite corner, teenagers mostly. They were singing "Have Yourself a Merry Little Christmas." Whatever happened to the classic Christmas carols — "Silent Night" and "O Little Town of Bethlehem"? Nothing was what it was supposed to be these days. Nothing worked right.

He would have to fix things, that was all.

He remembered the look on Bonnie's

face when she finally told him Tommy wasn't at home. Sad, pathetic, desperate. No doubt in his mind — she was telling the truth.

But if he wasn't home, where was he? Neither he nor Bonnie had parents living in the area.

Day care? It was pretty pathetic, thinking she would put the kid in day care on Christmas Eve, but that had to be the answer. He knew the private school she sent Tommy to provided child care during nonschool hours.

He shook his head. What a sorry thing to do. She probably wanted Tommy out of her hair. Probably just wanted him gone so she could celebrate the holidays one-on-one with Frank. How sick, and . . . and . . .

And how interesting. How interesting.

He zipped up his coat and headed down the street where he had parked his pickup. I will not let Christmas pass without seeing my son, he told himself. I will not allow that to happen. It isn't right.

He sucked in the bracing air, letting it swirl in his throat and lungs with the last traces of whiskey. I will see Tommy, he muttered resolutely. No matter what.

I will see Tommy.

Or no one will.

4

Megan fingered the small cameo-encased photograph. My dear sweet mother, she thought, as she had every day for weeks now. Who would have ever thought I could miss you so? When you were alive, it seemed like all we ever did was argue. And now that you're gone, I feel like someone cut a hole in my chest and ripped my heart out.

She turned down the photo and forced herself to look away. It wasn't healthy, she told herself. All this moaning and whining. Especially on Christmas Eve. The holidays were tough enough on a single woman without this kind of self-indulgence.

But that was the head talking, not the heart. The heart was telling her that her mother, her only family, was dead, and that she would spend Christmas Eve alone.

A growling, spitting noise erupted from the corner of her office. Jasper scooted forward and wiped his wet face against her exposed ankles.

Yes, she would be spending Christmas Eve alone. Or worse.

Her hand pressed against her forehead. How could this happen? How could she let it happen?

I'm all alone, she whispered quietly to herself. I'm all alone.

Before she had gone to law school, Megan had been an Episcopal priest. Technically she still was, she supposed, but people rarely thought of priests and lawyers as inhabiting the same body. During her eight years at St. Paul's, she had comforted any number of lonely and despondent persons, patted their hands, said the words they needed to hear. But today those words held no meaning for her. She just didn't believe them anymore.

Not now. Not after April 19, 1995.

Without thinking, her eyes rose to the row of ceramic Kewpie dolls lined up on a shelf just above her law books. The hula girl. The Eskimo. All the others.

So many memories. So many times shared.

And all of that was over now.

She sat up in her chair and scanned the cluttered surface of her desk. What was she doing here in the office, anyway? She had meant to stop in for only a minute to pick up a few things, since she was downtown anyway after finishing her cookie deliveries. There was no reason for her to stay.

But the sad thing was, there was no reason for her to go home, either.

She heard a knock on the door. A familiar head poked through. "Is Santa in?"

Megan looked up and tried to smile. "Ho, ho, ho."

Cindy Kendall strolled into Megan's office. She was tall, with shoulder-length ink-black hair and legs that went on to infinity. She was wearing a dignified but attractive beige suit — a Harold's special, probably. She looked like a million bucks, Megan thought, which was a value of roughly $999,999.00 more than Megan would've appraised herself.

Megan rose from her chair. "What's happening, Cindy-Lou Who?"

"Just came by to see if you finished the cookie rounds. Looks like you did. And survived to tell the tale."

Megan smiled. She liked Cindy a lot, even if she was devastatingly attractive. Whenever the teenage boys who worked in the firm as clerks ran their errands, they invented excuses to linger in Cindy's office. Megan was lucky if she got her morning mail.

"Completed my appointed rounds, and with no injury to self or others, I'm proud to say. Even made a bit of profit."

"Don't tell me one of those pro bono buddies paid you."

"In a way." Megan pointed toward the picture frame leaning face forward against the wall. "See for yourself."

Cindy took a step toward the picture, but Jasper scooted forward on his hindquarters and began howling. Spittle flew in all directions.

Cindy quickly backed away. "I'm sorry, Megan, but you have to get rid of this purported canine."

"I suppose in his own way he thinks he's protecting me."

"In his own way he is, but it's disgusting and he still has to go."

"Easy to say. But what can I do?"

"Call the dogcatcher. Send him to the vet for a lethal injection. Ship him to one of those third world nations where they have a meat shortage."

Megan covered her mouth. "Cindy! You're terrible!"

"Wimp." Cindy stepped around the dog, lifted the picture frame, and turned it around. "Oh my gosh."

"Isn't it awful?"

"No! It's wonderful!"

Megan blinked. "It is?"

"Yes!" Cindy held the picture in both hands. "Look at those cute widdle puppy dogs! Don't you just love it?"

"Cindy, it's kitsch."

"Yes, but it's classic kitsch." She laid the black-velvet masterwork on Megan's desk. "Seriously, Arnie is crazy about this kind of stuff. This is just what he's been needing for the pool room. You don't suppose . . ."

Megan waved her hand magnanimously. "It's yours."

"Oh, thank you! This is a Christmas gift he won't be expecting." She pressed her hand against her lips. "Oh! But I don't have anything for you!"

"That's quite all —"

"I'll be right back." Cindy scurried out of the office, then reappeared barely thirty seconds later. She plopped her treasure in the center of Megan's desk. "My mother-in-law gave me this last Christmas. Lovely woman, but . . ."

"What is it?" Megan asked. It was a small contraption, maybe half the size of a shoebox. It held five metal ball bearings hanging in a row, each suspended by two wires, one on either end, from the wooden framework. "What's it called?"

"Well . . ." Cindy hedged. "I don't really know what it's called."

"What does it do?"

"Watch." Cindy raised the ball bearing closest to her, then released it. The metal ball swung like a pendulum into the other four balls, which then kicked up together, hit the apex of their arc, then swung back into the other ball, which then swung up and back into the four balls, which then . . ."

"Okay," Megan said. "What next?"

"Whaddya mean, what next? There is no what next. That's it."

"That's it?"

"Right."

Megan nodded. "Um . . . thanks."

"You'll probably want to keep it in your office."

"Sure. Next to the lava lamp."

"Whatever." She snapped her fingers. "I almost forgot why I came in here. There's a new client waiting in the lobby —"

"On Christmas Eve?"

"She says it's an emergency. Of course, since I'm supposed to be handling the domestic cases now, they sent her to me, but

I haven't even finished my Christmas shopping, and if I don't get out of here soon I never will. I wouldn't do this to you normally, Megan, but there aren't many lawyers in the office today, and since . . . you know . . ."

Megan did know. What Cindy was saying but not saying was — Since you're not going anywhere, since you don't have anyone to see or to spend the holiday with —

". . . I wondered if you wouldn't mind talking to her."

"What does she need?"

"Emergency restraining order. Ex-husband."

Megan shrugged. "Cakewalk. Send her in."

"Thanks. I really appreciate it." She stopped at the door. "You know, Arnie and I are driving to Tulsa to spend Christmas with his folks. It's a two-hour drive, but if you're free by then, we'd love to have you —"

Megan smiled. "Thanks, Cindy. You're a good friend. But I have plans."

"You do?"

Granted, it was a lie, but Megan still wished Cindy didn't look quite so astonished. "I do." She winked. "Me and Jasper.

Now get out of here."

"Okay. Thanks so much, Megan." She hesitated. "Merry Christmas."

Megan nodded. "And to you."

Megan took advantage of the break to change out of her Santa suit and back into her standard-issue office clothes. About a minute later, the client in question entered Megan's office — a thin, petite woman. She had a fragile look about her, especially now, when her hands were trembling and her eyes were streaked and red from crying. Still, she was quite attractive. Maybe not in the Cindy Kendall million-dollar-model category, especially at the moment, but still, Megan thought, several G-notes ahead of me.

"I'm Bonnie Cantrell," she managed. She saw her hands shaking, then lowered them to her side. "I'm sorry. I guess I'm nervous. I've been so scared."

Megan reached out and steadied the woman's arm. "Just relax, please. Whatever's happened, I'm sure there's a solution. My associate told me you'd like a restraining order."

She nodded. Fresh tears leaked from her eyes. "It's Carl, my ex-husband."

Megan nodded sympathetically. "How

long have you been divorced?"

"More than two years now. I got custody. He didn't even get visitation rights. He —" She lowered her head. "He had a drinking problem. Has, I should say."

"I'm sorry. That must've been very difficult for you." More than once during her days at St. Paul's, Megan had counseled parents and spouses dealing with alcoholism. She knew it could have a devastating impact on the life of a family.

"It . . . was." Bonnie licked her lips, took a deep breath. "He never managed to succeed at anything. I tried to help but nothing ever seemed to work. I thought it would be better, after the divorce. But he's continued to harass us, to stalk me, my little boy."

"How old is your son?"

"Tommy's seven. Too young to understand why . . ." — another deep breath — "why his mommy doesn't want him to see his daddy."

"Have you called the police?"

Bonnie opened her purse and removed a stained handkerchief. "You have to understand — Carl is a cop."

Uh-oh. Megan fell back in her chair. This was going to be more complicated than she realized.

"He's not on active duty right now. He was suspended some time ago. But all the local cops know us. They consider Carl one of them. And they consider me someone who betrayed one of them."

"Still, you should lodge a complaint if he's threatening you. The law requires the police to —"

"I did call once. But Carl shaped up as soon as he heard the sirens. The cops hassled me, then wrote me a citation because the inspection sticker on my car had expired."

Megan's lips pursed.

"I'm just afraid if I call them again, they might do something horrible — like plant some cocaine in my bedroom. And then I'd be the one who goes to jail. And I'd lose custody of Tommy."

Megan laid her hand on Bonnie's. "I understand. So you want a restraining order. We'll go to the courthouse immediately. One of the judges is on duty today, handling emergency cases. We won't be able to get a permanent restraint without giving your ex notice and a chance to be heard, but we will be able to get a temporary order pending a later hearing. Of course we'll have to demonstrate that there are exigent circumstances."

"He came to the house today." Bonnie's voice cracked; she appeared to be on the verge of breaking down altogether. "The sun was barely up, but he was already drunk. Crazy drunk. Crazy mean drunk. He punched a friend of mine for no reason. He shoved a neighbor down the porch steps. He broke a window with his bare fist."

Megan gasped.

"I have witnesses. My neighbors saw everything. I can give you their names."

"Surely you called the police."

"One of the neighbors did. Carl ran off when he heard the sirens. I hid, let the neighbors talk to the police. I didn't want them to know it was me."

"That must've been awful. I'm so sorry." She placed her arm around Bonnie's shoulders and squeezed. As others had noted before, whether Megan's name was followed by D.D. or Esq., her counseling technique didn't change much.

"It was," Bonnie whispered. "It was a nightmare." She clutched her handkerchief so tightly she could have wrung water from it. "I was so scared. I'm still scared."

"Scared that he'll come back?"

"Scared of what he might do. Especially if he gets to Tommy."

"Surely he wouldn't hurt his own son."

Bonnie's eyes widened impossibly, and the flood of tears continued. "I know Carl. He's thinking, If I can't have Tommy, no one can."

A hollow ache resounded in the pit of Megan's stomach. It was a feeling she had learned to trust. "Forgive me for asking, Bonnie, but where's Tommy now?"

"He's at his school — it's a private school. Villa Veronica. I didn't want to bring him here. Didn't want him to see me like this."

"I don't want to alarm you," Megan said evenly, "but I think you should call. Right now." She yanked her cordless phone out of its cradle and passed it to Bonnie. "Just to check."

Bonnie nodded. Slowly, with trembling hands, she punched seven numbers onto the keypad.

A moment later, Megan heard a click that told her someone had answered the phone. "H-hello. This is Bonnie Cantrell. I — I wanted to check on Tommy."

Megan looked away, but continued to listen. "Yes," she heard Bonnie say. "Yes." Then there was a sudden intake of air. *"What?"*

Megan whirled around. "What is it? What happened?"

Bonnie looked up wordlessly. The phone fell out of her hands and landed on the carpet with a thud. "He isn't there."

"Isn't there? How can that be?"

Her answer was more whispered than spoken. "They say his father picked him up."

5

Carl exited I-35 and pulled into the parking lot of the Toys "Я" Us near Crossroads Mall. He was worried about Tommy. It had been a cinch liberating him from Villa Veronica. The permanent staff was off for the holidays and the substitutes were clueless. Why shouldn't he take Tommy? they thought. He was the boy's father, after all.

Carl had taken Tommy straight from the school to his car, but ever since then, Tommy had been almost motionless, sitting in the passenger seat staring out the window. No matter what ploy Carl tried to engage him in conversation, Tommy remained silent.

He supposed he shouldn't be surprised. The boy had barely seen him these past years. Once they had been as close as any two buddies on the face of the earth, but that was a long time ago now. Baby days, to a mature man of seven. He probably didn't even remember.

Damn that woman! She had no right to take his son away from him. She had no right to erect a wall between them. God only knew what horrible things she'd been telling Tommy about him. No wonder he didn't speak, didn't seem comfortable. She had probably turned his father into the biggest bogeyman who ever walked the earth. Probably maligned him while glorifying that sorry SOB she was with now.

"Damn!" he shouted aloud, pounding his fist on the dash.

He froze, suddenly embarrassed. His son was watching him. Not staring, but surreptitiously peering at him out of the corner of his eye.

Way to go, Carl, he swore silently to himself. The boy was already uncomfortable and confused. Now you've managed to totally alienate him.

It's too late. He tried to block out the thought, but it kept coming just the same. It's too late to undo all the damage she's done. He will never be yours again. Not unless you take him away from her. Not unless you take him away for good.

He parked the car, trying to quash the fears that haunted him. "Let's get out of the car," he growled.

He slid out of the seat. As he slammed the door, he noticed his son hadn't budged. "Well, are you coming already?" he said, waving his hands in the air.

Tommy popped the door open.

Carl shook his head. It seemed like only yesterday he had held this boy in his arms and rocked him to sleep. Now the kid came up to his waist. He had a thick thatch of jet-black hair that whipped across his head and hung lopsided over one side of his face. That was the fashion these days, he supposed, stupid-looking as it was. He decided not to make a fuss, even if it did make the kid look like a sissy. His whole face seemed round and soft; obviously his mother had been pampering him, treating him like a baby doll instead of a real boy, exposing him to weak-kneed influences like that boyfriend —

He stopped himself. He had to get out of this, had to concentrate on his son. He'd gone to all this trouble to get the kid; he should start taking advantage. Especially since he knew their time was limited.

They started across the parking lot. He reached for his son's hand, but the boy pulled away. "So what're you wanting for Christmas this year, son?"

The boy didn't look at him. "Mama says Santa will bring what I want tomorrow."

Carl rolled his eyes. The kid was seven and he still believed in Santa. Pampered. And he thinks he's going to get everything he wants. Spoiled.

"There must be something else you want. Something they don't have at the North Pole."

Tommy's head twitched a bit, though he still didn't make eye contact. "Mighty Movin' Dino-Fighter," he mumbled.

"What was that? What did you say?"

Tommy shrugged. "One of the kids at school has a Mighty Movin' Dino-Fighter. With the Super-Explosive Power Pack. You know, like on the TV show."

"Oh, right," Carl feigned. "Like on the show."

" 'Course, that's Corey Chambers. He has everything."

"Oh. I thought you had everything."

Tommy shrugged. "Not like Corey Chambers does."

Carl smiled sympathetically. The kid was talking to him!

They stepped up on the curb. A would-be Santa stood in front of the entrance, ringing his bell and trying to persuade shoppers to toss their spare change into his big red cauldron. Carl brushed by him quickly. He didn't have any change to spare. The two electronic-eye doors slid open and he and Tommy entered the store.

Or tried, anyway. The place was jam-packed, so much so that they could barely make their way through the entry.

"What's going on here?" Carl said.

"It's Christmas Eve," Tommy explained.

"I know, but . . ." Carl tried to push his way forward, without much success. It was a madhouse. Bodies, carts, strollers blocked the aisles. People were tearing items off the shelves. Desperate expressions were plastered on the faces of adults as they struggled to reach the items they needed. There was kicking and shoving and a frequent exchange of very un-Christmas-like remarks. Pure pandemonium.

Tommy frowned. "We'll never get a Mighty Movin' Dino-Fighter. Let's get out of here."

"I'm not giving up that easily." Carl pushed his way forward, knocking people out of the way, while Tommy trailed behind in his wake. Someone shoved up against him on the right, sending a shock wave of pain through his body, reminding him that the wound on his arm had still not been treated.

He grabbed the first person he saw wearing a Toys "Я" Us name tag: CHERRI. She looked to be about fifteen. "Can you help me?"

"I'll try, sir," Cherri said, but her tone suggested that she was unlikely to put a lot of effort into the attempt. "What are you looking for?"

"We need a Mighty — Mighty —" He looked down. "What is it again, son?"

"Mighty Movin' Dino-Fighter," Tommy mumbled.

"That's it. We need a Mighty Movin' Dino-Fighter. The best one you've got."

Cherri's lips turned up at both ends and she began to laugh. "I'll bet you would," she said, laughing all the more. "You and everyone else in this store."

"You mean you don't have one? What kind of toy store is this?"

"Sir, the Dino-Fighter is the hit toy of the season. Everyone wants one, and we haven't had any since early November. We don't expect to have any until late January."

"But that doesn't do me any good. I need one now. For Christmas."

"Sorry, sir. No can do."

"Then we'll go somewhere else."

"You could go to every toy store in the

country, sir, but the story will be the same. They just aren't available."

Carl felt trapped. Here it was, starting all over again. No matter what he did, no one would help, no one would give him a break. No matter what he tried, he always came out a failure.

"You don't understand," he said slowly. "I *must* have that toy."

"I guess you don't understand," Cherri said, staring right back at him. Apparently the day's work had hardened her. "We don't have any!"

"Please," Carl said, his voice rising in volume, "I need a Mighty Movin' Dino-Fighter!"

All at once there was a break in the general pandemonium. A hush fell; the movement ceased.

One lone voice emerged from the back of the crowd. "You've got Mighty Movin' Dino-Fighters?"

Cherri held up her hands. "No, no," she said quickly. "You misunder—"

But it was too late.

"They've got Dino-Fighters!" a woman cried. "Fred! Over here! *Dino-Fighters!*"

If the store had been in chaos before, it was in Armageddon now. All at once, every warm body in the store bolted toward

Cherri and Carl. They were screaming and pushing and fighting to get to the front. Cherri barricaded herself behind the customer service counter, but the horde continued surging forward. Their hands stretched over the counter, grasping at air.

"Do you have the Power Packs?" one voice demanded. "I want three!" shouted another. "I have to have *three!*"

"I'm telling you, we're sold out!" Cherri said, but no one was listening. They were an unreasoning mob acting with a single purpose.

"Let's get out of here," Carl said, recognizing the futility of continuing this particular fight. He reached out his hand, but of course, Tommy didn't take it. The two of them forced their way to the exits.

They returned to Carl's pickup. Carl jumped behind the wheel, while Tommy resumed his previous sullen posture in the passenger seat, staring out the window.

"I'm . . . um . . . sorry about that, son," Carl said finally.

"It's okay," Tommy said. This time he didn't even bother to shrug. "It's no big deal. I knew you couldn't get a Mighty Movin' Dino-Fighter."

Of course not, Carl thought. His brain boiled with rage. Of course not. Not your stupid, useless, impotent father. He can't do anything right. He fails at everything. That's what she's told you, isn't it? That's what she's made you believe.

He started the car and pulled out of the parking lot, driving much too fast. He'd had it with that woman, that ugly woman and all the venom she spewed, even to his own son. She'd poisoned his mind for good. There was nothing he could do, he realized now. No way he could bring Tommy back. No way he could make his son his again.

"Let's get something to eat," Carl said, pulling back onto I-35.

"Everything good'll be closed," Tommy mumbled.

"I know a place," Carl replied. And he did, too. He knew a perfect place. Especially for today.

There were no more options open to him, he realized. No way to make things like they were before. There was only one opportunity before him now. Only one choice.

They would go for lunch, Carl resolved. They would go out together one last time.

And then he would remove the boy from his mother's evil grasp for good.

6

"How could you let him take away my Tommy?" Bonnie shrieked.

The caregiver tried to remain calm. "I'm sorry, I didn't know —"

"You should've known!"

"No one told me anything, ma'am. I can assure you that if they had —"

"I don't want to hear any more of your excuses!"

Megan laid her hand on Bonnie's shoulder, trying to calm her and subtly signal her to cool off. The situation was dire enough already. They needed to keep their heads together and figure out what to do next.

Megan's heart also went out to the poor caregiver, the dark-haired woman who had drawn the thankless duty of administering the short staff on Christmas Eve. She could never have anticipated that she would be thrust in the middle of a horrible domestic crisis.

Bonnie looked a wreck; her face was streaked with tears and ruined makeup. Megan knew fear was eating away at her, fears she hadn't even expressed but were haunting her just the same.

"How could you let that man take my son? I left specific instructions that he not be allowed anywhere near my Tommy. There is a copy of the divorce decree in the files!"

"I'm sorry, ma'am. I didn't know any of that."

"So you just let anyone stroll in and walk away with the children?"

"Of course not, ma'am. He wasn't just anyone. He was Tommy's father. Tommy confirmed that. And he had identification. Plus he showed us a lot of very official-looking papers."

"He used to be a cop!" Bonnie shouted. "He has a glove box full of official-looking papers."

Megan took a step forward, hoping that Bonnie would catch her breath and let someone else take the lead for a bit. The caregiver was behaving admirably; even under fire she was staying cool. But Megan knew that wouldn't last forever.

"There's no point in beating this dead horse," Megan said in a quiet but firm voice. "He has Tommy. We need to figure out where they've gone. Did you by any chance notice what kind of car he was driving?"

Concentration lines etched the caregiver's face. "I think it was blue. No, wait. Red."

"Are you sure?"

"I think so. Yes. Red."

"What kind of car?"

She frowned. "Gee, I'm really not good with cars."

"Two-door or four?"

"Four. No, two. Actually — come to think of it, he may have been driving a pickup."

"I don't suppose you noticed the license plate?"

The caregiver shook her head.

"He drove a red pickup when we were married," Bonnie said softly. "It was a heap, but he seemed to like it. He probably still has it."

"That's something, then." Megan turned back to the caregiver. "Did he say where he was taking Tommy?"

"Not exactly. But he did say something about buying a Christmas present."

Bonnie frowned. "Him and everyone else on earth today."

"And I think he mentioned getting something to eat."

"Did he say where they might go?" Megan asked.

"He asked Tommy where he wanted to go."

Megan leaned in anxiously. "And what did Tommy say?"

"He didn't. Didn't answer. You know, he didn't really seem all that happy about going."

Bonnie's eyes flew open, her face livid. "Then why in the name of —"

Megan stopped her from finishing the sentence. "Excuse me. I'd like to speak to my client." She tugged Bonnie toward the front door. "Thank you for your help, ma'am. We'll get back to you soon."

Once they were outside, Bonnie whirled on her. "Why did you stop me from —"

"Because it wasn't doing us any good. Us or Tommy. And we don't have time for it." She took Bonnie's hand and squeezed it. "I know how distraught you are. It's affecting your judgment."

Bonnie's head fell. "You're right." She inhaled deeply. "What do we do now?"

"First we call the police."

"Of course. I didn't even think —"

"Then we start cruising all the malls and

toy stores and shopping centers. I know it's a long shot, but if you remember your ex-husband's pickup, it's just possible you'll spot it."

Bonnie shook her head slowly from side to side. Tears welled up in her eyes. "We won't be quick enough. We won't find him in time."

Megan tried to use a gentle tone. "Bonnie, I think you should prepare yourself for the possibility that Tommy might not be with you for Christmas. I know that's tough, but —"

Tears spilled down Bonnie's face. "You don't understand," she whispered, her voice broken. "You don't understand."

Megan tried. "You're afraid he'll kidnap Tommy. Take him away somewhere."

"More than that." Her voice dropped. "You remember what I said before. How Carl feels. How selfish he is. How he thinks if he can't have Tommy, no one can."

Megan's throat suddenly went dry. "Are you saying — ?"

Bonnie nodded, shaking tears down her cheeks. "He'll kill him," she whispered. "I know he will."

"But he's the boy's father! How can you think that?"

Bonnie looked up, her face red and ruined. "Because he's tried before."

Carl stared across the car at his son, so young, so tiny, so fragile. So easily hurt.

He pulled his eyes to the front. First things first. He had promised this boy lunch. So lunch it would be.

The sky was even darker than before. It was going to snow today; he was sure of it. Best to get inside beforehand.

He took the Western exit and wove through the heavy traffic. There was an Asian restaurant, The Snow Pea, just a short hop from the Cowboy Hall of Fame. It would be the perfect place for lunch.

He pulled his pickup into the parking lot and turned off the ignition. "How's this look, champ?"

Tommy glanced up at the front of the restaurant and shrugged. "Whatever."

"You like Chinese, don't you? Stir-fry?"

"Fine."

"If there's something else you'd rather have —"

"No. This is fine." He opened the car door and slithered out of the car. Carl followed.

The restaurant was decked out in glittery silver and gold tinsel. There was a

Christmas tree in the corner with presents (probably empty) artfully arranged beneath. Muzaked carols played through overhead speakers. What was that one? Carl gritted his teeth. "Have Yourself a Merry Little Christmas." He was learning to hate that song.

They found a table and ordered. Carl went for the lo mein noodles; Tommy finally selected the spicy chicken with peanuts. They got Cokes from the dispenser and sat down.

"This probably isn't very Christmassy," Carl said. "We'll do better tonight."

Tommy looked up. "I thought I was spending tonight with Mommy. And Frank."

"Is that what you want?"

"That's what she told me we were going to do."

"Uh-huh. And what did she tell you I was going to do on Christmas Eve?"

His son looked at him blankly.

Carl's hand tightened around his fork. Damn that woman and her poison. Damn her and her lies. Damn her and what she had done to this family.

He had hoped they could at least get through Christmas, at least spend the day together, before Tommy went back to his mother. But now he saw that was impossible. The woman had done her venomous work too thoroughly. He had no time, no alternatives, no choices left to him.

He would prove to her that he wasn't a total loser, that he could accomplish something. This time he would finish the job. He would finish what he had tried to do before. He would prove to his ex-wife that he wasn't a failure at everything.

Then the conversation would be over. Permanently.

7

"He was always abusive," Bonnie said in a hoarse whisper. Her hands drummed nervously against the passenger door of Megan's Toyota. "Verbally. He could be so cruel. And when he lost his temper . . . well . . . sometimes he hit me. Hit me hard. But that was nothing compared to what happened toward the end."

Megan kept her eyes on the road. "What happened?"

"He was getting into trouble with his superiors on the police force. Drinking too much. Basically, he was destroying his life, and he knew it. So he took it out on us."

"You mean —"

"You know what I mean. Me and Tommy."

Megan nodded grimly. They were cruising through the parking lot at Penn Square Mall, hoping to bring in a long shot. It was just possible that Carl would bring Tommy toy-shopping here, and that Bonnie might recognize the pickup. They had already called the police, who had promised to do everything they could, but given the circumstances — that Tommy hadn't been gone long, that he was with his father, that it was Christmas Eve — that probably wouldn't be much. Bonnie had nearly collapsed with hysteria; Megan had promised they would do everything they could think of to find the boy themselves.

"Did he . . . hit Tommy?" Megan asked.

"He tried once. The night before I finally left him. I'll never forget that night. He came home livid, seething with rage. And stinking drunk. He was striking out at everything within reach. Tommy did something — I don't even remember what. Didn't matter — it was just an excuse. Carl reared up his fist and" — Bonnie covered her face with her hands — "I just thank God I was there. I pulled him out of the way. Told him to go to bed." Her lips pressed tightly together. "Of course, after I did that, you can guess who became Target Number One."

"He beat you?"

"Not at first. At first we just shouted insults at each other. I told him I was going to divorce him. He didn't care. But then I told him I was going to take Tommy away from him. That's when he went ballistic. Screaming, hitting. Said he would never let anyone take his son away from him. Said he'd kill him first."

Megan's stony demeanor was rapidly fading. "What did he do then?"

"Then he became violent. Physically violent."

Megan swallowed. "How violent?"

Bonnie's eyes took on a glassy, fixed cast. "Like you wouldn't believe. I — I had heard stories about women — about —" She took a deep breath. "About battered women. But I never imagined. He hit me in the face — blackened both eyes. He cracked a collarbone. Bruised my arms, legs, breasts. Bleeding. I was a mess."

Her head sunk low, as if the shame of the memory still haunted her. "I felt like I'd been crippled, in every way you can imagine. I just lay there on the floor in the living room, whimpering, barely breathing, unable to move. Finally, I guess it wasn't fun for him anymore, punching an inanimate object. He ran off, probably to some bar. I can't tell you how relieved I was. I — I really thought he was going to kill me."

Megan kept staring straight ahead,

trying not to react. "And that was when you left him?"

"Actually, no. Pretty pathetic, huh? No, even after that, I didn't have the guts to make the move. I just lay on the floor for what seemed like an eternity until I heard Tommy coming down the stairs. He was still awake, you see. He'd seen the whole thing. I was so ashamed." She covered her face with her hands.

"Was he . . . upset?"

"He was very subdued. Amazingly mature, all things considered. He knew I was hurt. He kept saying, 'Come on, Mommy. Let's go to the hospital.' So I finally pulled myself together and went to the hospital. That's when they told me I had a fractured collarbone."

"And that's when you decided to leave him."

Bonnie let out a laugh, a small bitter laugh. "No, not even then. Not even then." She raised her head, wiping her eyes clear. "Truth is, I didn't know what to do. Didn't have a clue. So we went home. Carl wasn't there, so we both went upstairs to our rooms. I collapsed on the bed, fell asleep. Didn't wake up for twelve hours."

"You must've been exhausted."

"I was." There was a long pause. The

tremble returned to her voice. "But when I woke up, Carl was home. With Tommy."

Megan shook her head, too horrified to make an intelligent comment. "What did you do?"

"At first, nothing. It seemed innocent enough. They were sitting at the breakfast table together, eating cereal. Carl didn't appear drunk. He wasn't raving or lashing out. I had a headache like you wouldn't believe. So I poured myself some juice and sat at the table with them."

"As if nothing had happened."

"That's exactly right. As if he hadn't tried to obliterate me the night before." She took a deep breath, tried to steady herself. "Tommy was about to take his first bite before I noticed."

"Noticed . . . what?"

"There was something powdery all over his cornflakes. And it wasn't sugar frosting, either. It was rat poison."

Megan's foot slammed down on the brake. "Rat poison?"

Bonnie nodded. "You see, he had meant what he said. Every word of it. If he couldn't have Tommy, no one could. And the thing is . . . the thing is . . ."

Her body began to quiver, consumed by anguish and fear. "The thing is . . ." she repeated, her voice choking, "he said the same thing this morning."

"Eat your food," Carl said.

Tommy pushed the spicy chicken with peanuts away. "I'm not hungry."

"Here, I've got a little something that will make it especially good." He poured a dark liquid over the food, then stirred it in. "You'll really like this. I want you to eat every bite." He looked steadily into Tommy's eyes. "You understand me? Every single bite."

8

"Please hurry," Bonnie said. She was practically edging out of the car seat. "I have the worst feeling about this. We have to hurry."

But Megan did not accelerate. They were negotiating the densely packed parking lot at Quail Springs Mall, and high speed was not an option.

"Don't you hear me?" Bonnie's voice was becoming shrill in its desperation. "We have to hurry!"

Megan stopped the car. She had hoped to postpone this discussion as long as possible, but the truth was, Bonnie was practically over the brink. Her fear was making her irrational.

"Bonnie, listen to me. I know how frightened you are. But the fact is, we've cruised every parking lot we could think of —"

"Don't you understand? He's insane! He's going to try to kill my Tommy! We have to hurry!"

"Bonnie, listen! There's no point in hurrying unless we have somewhere to hurry to!"

Bonnie fell silent. Megan seized the opportunity.

"We've tried every mall. We didn't find him. Even if he was at one, he would've left by now. We have to come up with a new plan. Can you think of anywhere else they might go?"

Bonnie shrugged. Megan could see she was trying to regain control, trying to put her brain back in order. "I don't know where he lives now."

"And neither do the police. What else?"

"He has a cellular phone he carries. He gave me the number."

"And you called it. No answer. What else?"

Bonnie shrugged helplessly. "I — I don't know . . ."

Megan glanced at her watch. "It's about lunchtime. Is there someplace special they might go for lunch?"

Bonnie's eyes darted around the small car, as if the answers might be written somewhere on the upholstery. "I don't know."

"Think, Bonnie. Think. Does Tommy have a favorite place?"

Bonnie continued shaking her head.

"McDonald's? Burger King? Split-T?"

"No, he doesn't like any of —" She froze abruptly. "Oh, my — it's Christmas Eve! I didn't even think."

"What? What is it?"

"Christmas Eve. It's a special day."

"Right. Major holiday. Santa Claus and ho-ho-ho."

Bonnie shook her head. "More than that. It's our wedding anniversary. We were married on Christmas Eve. Nine years ago today. No wonder he's flown off his rocker. He must've remembered."

"You were married on Christmas Eve?"

"Right here in OKC." She snapped her fingers. "And after the ceremony, we ate at The Snow Pea."

Megan did a double take. "The Chinese place?"

"Right. The one on Western. I know it seems crazy, but I just wonder if —"

She didn't even have to finish the sentence. Megan had already thrown the transmission into Drive. The car lurched forward as she began weaving her way out of the overcrowded parking lot.

Now at last they had someplace they could go in a hurry.

"Tommy, I want you to eat your food."

Tommy folded his arms across his chest. "I'm not hungry."

"Just a few bites, then. For me."

Tommy looked away, sullen-faced. "Mommy says I shouldn't eat when I'm not hungry. She says it starts a bad habit."

"That's what this is all about, isn't it? Your mother. She always comes between us."

"She just doesn't want me to get fat. Like this kid in my class, Jerry Douglas. He's a real tub, and —"

"She can't even allow me one little bit of pleasure, can she? Can't give me one last moment of peace with my son."

Tommy didn't answer.

Carl leaned across the table. "Listen to me, Tommy. I'm your father. I held you in my arms when you were just a baby. I was there the day you were born. I'm your friend."

"Does Mommy know where I am?"

The question caught Carl by surprise. "She . . . knows you're with me. I'm sure of that."

"Does she know where I am?"

"Well . . . in general. She may not know precisely —"

"Are you kidnapping me?"

Pound, pound, pound. The kid kept

pounding him with questions. He was almost as bad as his mother. Was there no escaping them? "Tommy, what are you saying? You're my son."

"Fathers kidnap their sons sometimes. I read about it in the *Weekly Reader.* Is that what you're doing?"

Carl pressed his hands against the table. "All I'm doing right now is having a nice Christmas Eve lunch with my son. The only problem is, you're not eating!"

Tommy sank back in his chair.

"So eat already, would you? It's important!"

"Why?"

"It —" He checked himself. "It just is, all right? So eat."

"I'm not hungry."

Carl swelled with rage. He reached across the table, grabbed Tommy's spoon, and shoveled up a heaping spoonful of chicken with peanuts. "I'm your father, Tommy. You're supposed to do what I say. Do you understand me? So you *will* eat your dinner." His eyes twitched. "If it's the last thing you do."

9

"Eat!" Carl shouted. *"Eat!"*

Tommy pushed his plate away. "I don't want to. You can't make me!"

"You're my son!" Carl glanced around the room. They were beginning to attract the attention of the handful of other patrons, as well as the Asian woman behind the cash register. "Do as you're told!"

"I'm not going to!"

"Don't be a bad boy, Tommy!" He grabbed Tommy by the neck and jerked him forward, pressing the spoon against his lips. "Eat!"

"Don't do it, Tommy!"

Carl's head jerked up. God in heaven — it was Bonnie! Bonnie and some other woman he didn't know. Somehow they'd managed to find him.

He dropped the spoon. It clattered to the floor as he leapt out of his chair.

"Someone please help!" Bonnie cried.

"Someone arrest him! Call the police! They're looking for him!"

"Bonnie — baby —"

"Grab the food!" Bonnie lurched forward and pushed the plate away from Tommy. "Tommy, did you eat any of it? Did you eat anything?"

"No, Mommy. I —"

"Oh, thank God." She threw her arms around him and hugged him close against her chest. "Did someone call the police?"

Carl saw that the woman behind the register was talking quietly into the phone. "Bonnie, you can't do this. I was just having lunch with my son. It's Christmas Eve!"

"You sick creep, you were trying to kill him. Would someone *please* arrest him!"

Carl pushed away from the table and grabbed Tommy by the shirt. "I'm taking the boy with me."

"Like hell," Bonnie answered.

"You can't stop me," he growled.

"What are you going to do? Beat me up again? Fracture my collarbone?"

Carl's face twisted. "What? Bonnie, it doesn't have to be like this!" He saw one of the other diners, a large heavyset man in his early thirties, inching forward. He knew he had to move quickly or he would encounter some serious resistance. "This isn't over, Bonnie. Not by a long shot." He turned quickly and fled out the front door.

Megan tried to stop Carl as he rushed past, but he knocked her out of the way without even breaking his stride. She pushed herself back to her feet, but by the time she had raced outside, Carl was speeding away in his red pickup. She did manage to get the license-plate number, though: XAU-208. She scribbled it down on a scrap of paper, then ran back inside the restaurant.

"Did someone call the —" She stopped. Bonnie was cradling her son in her arms, pressing him against her chest.

"Oh, God," she kept murmuring under her breath. "Oh, thank you, God."

A nod from the woman behind the counter told Megan the police were on their way. She plopped herself into the nearest chair, suddenly exhausted. She leaned forward and laid her head on the table.

She would have to pull herself together before the police arrived. Someone had to bring them up-to-date, and she could hardly expect Bonnie to do it. The police had to understand what was happening.

Even if Carl was an ex-cop, they had to try to find the man. Before he returned.

She was glad they'd found Tommy before it was too late. But her elation hadn't made her forget what Carl had said before he bolted out the door.

This isn't over, Bonnie, he said.

And as Megan stared into the man's steely eyes, she knew he meant it. She knew this wasn't over.

She knew he'd be back.

10

Megan assured Bonnie they were perfectly safe in her office. Security guards controlled the access to the elevators, and security cameras were everywhere. But it didn't seem to matter. No matter what she said, Bonnie continued to cling tightly to her son.

"I'm just so relieved," she kept murmuring, over and over again. "So grateful."

Megan couldn't help but smile. She was relieved, too. The whole time they had scoured the parking lots, she had known in her heart they were chasing a long shot of the tallest order. She did it mostly just to calm Bonnie, to make her feel as if they were trying. She had never in a million years expected it to bear fruit. When they finally did manage to track down Tommy, and just in the nick of time, it seemed like a miracle of the highest order.

Miracle. Now that was a funny thought.

Especially from someone who didn't seem to believe in much of anything these days.

Speaking of miracles, Jasper had finally settled down in the corner of her office. When she had first come in with Bonnie and Tommy, he had gone into attack mode. What exactly he thought he was going to do to them wasn't clear — drool them to death, maybe. At any rate, Megan had fed him, calmed him, and hooked his leash around her desk lamp. For the moment, he seemed content. When the occasional inevitable expulsions of gas were released, Bonnie simply pretended she hadn't heard. And Tommy . . . well, it was nice to finally see the boy crack a smile.

"I've talked to the police," Megan explained. Bonnie and Tommy were sharing a chair on the opposite side of the desk in her small office. "They've taken the food from the Chinese restaurant. They're going to run tests to see if" — she glanced quickly at Tommy — "well, you know."

Bonnie nodded. "I already know. I could see it the moment I looked into Carl's eyes."

"Well, after the tests, we'll know for sure. I also gave them Carl's license-plate number, and they promised to broadcast it to all the patrol cars in the area."

"Then they should pick him up soon," Bonnie said. "Lock him away. Make sure he doesn't try anything again."

"We can hope." Megan wasn't sure how to play it. She didn't want to destroy the tiny bit of hope in Bonnie's eyes. At the same time, it could be disastrous to lull her into a false sense of security. "The fact is, there's going to be a lot of traffic on the streets today, and the police can't possibly check everyone. Plus, I'm almost certain Carl saw me take down the license-plate number. He may be smart enough to ditch the truck."

Bonnie agreed. "He may be drunk and desperate, but he isn't stupid."

"That was my impression as well." Megan tried to lift the sudden gloom that had descended. "Still, the important thing is, you've got Tommy back. There's no reason why you shouldn't be able to have a very merry Christmas." She tried to put as much enthusiasm into this pronouncement as possible, but she observed very little change in Bonnie's demeanor. "The most important thing is, you're all safe."

"But for how long?" Bonnie asked. "I want a restraining order."

"Definitely." Megan glanced at her notepad. "And we're appearing before the emergency domestic judge in forty-five minutes. Given what I know, and what the police have on record, it should be a cinch. And after we serve notice on Carl and have a formal hearing, I see no problem with getting a permanent restraining order."

"Good. I don't want Carl near us. I don't want him anywhere in a ten-mile radius."

"You know, Bonnie . . ." Megan fingered the edge of her desk. It seemed she had nothing to bring but bad tidings this Christmas. But as an attorney, she had obligations — like the unpleasant duty to give her client a healthy dose of reality. "We'll get the restraining order. But when all is said and done, an order is just a piece of paper. Like any other law, it can be broken. Ultimately, it's only as effective as the police who enforce it."

"The police won't lift a finger against Carl."

"I'm not sure I believe that, Bonnie. Especially not now. But you should realize that if Carl really is desperate — a piece of paper isn't going to stop him."

"So what are you saying?"

"I'm saying I wouldn't necessarily stop with the restraining order. Maybe consider buying a big dog. A Doberman pinscher might slow Carl down."

"I can't do that." She pulled her boy closer to her. "Not with Tommy in the house."

"Perhaps a high-grade security system."

"We can't begin to afford that."

"Well, you need to do something. At least until Carl is safely behind bars."

Bonnie nodded, but Megan wasn't sure how much of this was sinking in. Bonnie was so overwhelmed with relief at having Tommy back, she didn't seem able to process any additional information.

"Do you mind if I ask you a question?" Bonnie asked, after a bit. "It . . . may be personal."

Megan's brow creased. She hadn't anticipated this. "Can't hurt to ask."

"You seem . . . very professional," she said haltingly. "Very lawyerly."

"Well, I try," Megan said, adjusting the collar on her gray skirt-suit.

"Everything in this office is just about as I would expect it to be. With two exceptions. First, this." She lifted the end ball bearing of Megan's new desk toy and let it slam into the rest of the ball bearings.

"That was a gift from my buddy Cindy. Sort of." Megan grabbed the toy and dropped it into her oversize purse. "Maybe

I'll give it to some needy person. Very needy."

"And the other anomaly," Bonnie continued, "is this." She pivoted slightly, then pointed to the long row of ceramic Kewpie dolls lined up on a shelf just over Megan's law books. "What's the story with the dolls?"

Megan smiled. "My mother made those. She took a ceramics class at OCU about a million years ago. Learned how to paint them, bake them in a kiln. For years afterward, she gave them to me as presents. I have a bunch more at home."

"I would never have guessed there was such a . . . wide variety of Kewpie dolls."

Megan laughed. "Or wanted to, right?" She walked over to the shelf. Each of the figures seemed to have the same wide, big-eyed face, with different apparel suggesting various locales. "Mother was a world traveler. She never had much money, but what little she could scrape together, she used to travel. When I was little, whenever she was getting ready to go away on a big trip, she would give me a present — one of these dolls."

Megan pointed to a well-tanned Kewpie on the top shelf wearing a hula skirt. "For instance, just before she left for two weeks in Hawaii, she gave me this hula one." She moved her finger down the row to a parka-wrapped figurine. "Sometimes she wrapped them up and left them for me to find after she was gone. A few days after she departed for her big cruise around Alaska, I found this furry Eskimo doll." She laughed. "Pretty cheesy, I know. But when I was a girl, I loved them. Actually, I still do."

"Your mother sounds like a sweet woman," Bonnie replied. "Does she live here in Oklahoma City?"

"Uh, no." Megan looked down abruptly. "She's . . . gone. Died not two months ago."

"Oh no. I'm so sorry."

Megan waved away the sympathy. She didn't want it. "It's all right. It was a long time coming."

"Had she been . . . very ill?"

Megan shrugged uncomfortably. "In a way. She was —" She took a deep breath. "She was in the Murrah building. The day the bomb exploded."

"Oh, my God." Bonnie's eyes widened with the memory of that tragic day. "Was she — ?"

"She worked for the Social Security Administration, on one of the upper levels. Her floor collapsed, smashing down on everything and everyone beneath. She was trapped under the rubble for more than ten hours."

Bonnie's chin dropped.

"All that time she lay helpless, pinioned, alone, trapped under the remains of her desk, listening to the sounds of her closest friends shrieking and crying. Dying." Megan lowered herself into a chair. "She was never the same after that. Physically, she recovered. But inside . . . never."

Bonnie shook her head, as if groping for something to say when there was simply nothing that could be said. "You must have been a great comfort to her, Megan. At least she had someone to talk to. Someone to help her through it. A daughter and a capable lawyer rolled into one."

Megan's face remained impassive. "Well, I wasn't a lawyer at the time. It was only after . . ." She stopped. There was no point in trying to explain. And no point in detailing those last dreadful months her mother spent in the hospital, so long and torturous that finally she told Megan she was ready to die. But Megan wasn't ready to let her go. She came to the hospital every day, begging her mother to hold on. Until finally, about two months ago, her mother called for her. But by the time

Megan arrived at the hospital, her mother was gone.

No, she thought silently. There was definitely no point in going into all that.

She pushed herself back to her feet. "Anyway, let me prepare you for —"

A knock at the door interrupted her. "Got a call from the courthouse," Cindy said to Megan. "You're on in thirty minutes."

"Great." Megan grabbed her briefcase and her shoulder bag. She gestured toward Bonnie. "I'll clue you in on the way to court."

Cindy started back out the door. "I'm off to shop till I drop. I really appreciate this."

"Don't worry. You'd do the same for me."

"It's still not too late," Cindy said. "We won't leave for Tulsa till five or so. If you'd like to join us —"

"No." Megan held up her hand. "Thanks, but I don't belong there. You have a great time."

"But who will you spend Christmas —"

"Please." Megan gently nudged her out of the doorway. "Enjoy yourselves. Merry Christmas."

"Merry Christmas," Cindy replied, but

Megan couldn't help but detect the note of sadness, of sympathy, in her voice. Exactly what she didn't want to hear.

"Come on then," Megan said, gathering Bonnie and Tommy. "We don't want to keep the judge waiting."

She ushered them out of the office. As she closed the office door, her eyes lighted once more on the row of Kewpie dolls on the back shelf. So many dolls representing so many excursions. So many years.

The truth is, after a while, she had gotten sick of the silly things. She had treated them scornfully, even made jokes to her friends about these stupid ugly dolls her mother kept making for her.

And now everything was different, wasn't it? Now, if she could have any Christmas gift in the whole wide world, she would wish for one more Kewpie doll.

From her mother.

Carl staggered down the streets of downtown Oklahoma City, wondering what to do next. In the past hour or so the sky had clouded up and it had become bitter cold. He crossed Robinson, then headed toward the Liberty Bank building. He had no idea what he would do there, but at least he could step in the alcove where they kept the ATM machines. That was still open.

He pushed through the swinging glass door, shivering. He wasn't dressed for this kind of weather. The wind was bracing, unforgiving, especially downtown. OKC was a windy city, even windier than Chicago. Most people didn't know that, but Carl did. Especially today, when every burst of cold air made him catch his breath. Worst of all, the cold seemed to exacerbate the aching in his arm. It had been different when he was with Tommy. Then he had focused all his attention on pleasing the boy, trying to make him happy. He had tried to forget about the pain, tried to forget about the deep gash that had practically torn his arm in half, but it wouldn't let him. The bleeding had stopped, thank God, but the pain hadn't.

He rolled up his sleeve and looked at it. It had matted into an ugly black mess. He wondered: could he get gangrene? Did people still die of things like that? He didn't know. He probably needed to have this looked at. But frankly, that wasn't an option at the moment. He had more urgent business.

As soon as he had gotten away from The Snow Pea, and he was certain no one was following him, he had ditched the truck.

He didn't know who the woman in the suit was, but he saw her write down his license-plate number. He could be absolutely certain the police had it by now. They'd be looking for him. From here on out, he had to make his way on foot.

Make his way where? That was the killing question. He had to get to Tommy, had to get him back. But how? He could be certain now that Bonnie wouldn't let him out of her sight. What was he going to do?

He needed inspiration. And the only way he knew to find inspiration was . . .

He pushed himself through the glass door, reentering the bracing cold. Yes! There it was, just down Main. Tony's Bar and Grill, except there was no grill, not that he'd ever noticed anyway. He used to be a regular, before he joined the force and —

Well, it didn't matter. He wasn't welcome at Joe's anymore, but no one at Tony's had a grudge against him. Not that he knew, anyway. And hallelujah! The place appeared to be open.

He pushed through the door, feeling the sudden rush of warmth and comfort. The smell of alcohol was thick in the air and it pleased him.

Maybe there were Christmas spirits, after all. He laughed. Maybe they were the kind of spirits you found in a bottle.

He sidled up to the bar and ordered. He felt better already. The pain was subsiding, his head was clearing, and ideas were flashing. Just another drink or two. Maybe three. Four at the most.

And then he felt confident he would know what to do next.

11

Megan had thought that perhaps, this being Christmas Eve, and everyone on earth having Christmassy activities to attend to, the county courthouse would be deserted. Wrong.

The courthouse was packed. Only one courtroom in the Family Division was open, only one judge was on duty, and roughly fifty billion people were jockeying for her attention. The small waiting room outside was jam-packed with mothers, fathers, and unhappy children who wanted to be anywhere but here on Christmas Eve. And of course each of them had a lawyer. Maybe two.

In short, it was a madhouse.

Megan found two seats in a relatively quiet corner and tucked Bonnie and Tommy away there. Before she had a chance to find a seat herself, her cell phone buzzed.

She pulled the phone out of her shoulder bag and flipped it open. "Megan McGee."

"This is Barney Palmer, over at the police station. Toxicology."

Megan glanced at Tommy out the corner of her eye. He was talking to his mother, unaware of what Megan was saying or doing.

She took a subtle step away and pressed the phone close against her ear. "Have you had a chance to test the food sample the police brought in?"

"Oh, yes. It's not a time-consuming process. Especially not with such a plentiful sample. Sergeant Conner asked me to phone you the results. I can fax a copy of the report to your office."

"That would be wonderful. But can you tell me over the phone?"

"You mean, the results?"

"Right. Was the food poisoned?"

She listened to several moments of staticky air. "I'm really not supposed to give this information out over the phone, but" — his voice dropped to a shadow of what it had been before — "the test was positive."

"You mean —"

"That's what I mean. The food was poisoned. Rat poison, we think. Enough to kill an elephant."

Megan felt as if her heart had been crushed in someone's fist. A cold chill rippled through her body. She had known all along that Carl was bad news, desperate, irrational. But somehow she had never quite believed he was capable of killing his own child.

Until now.

"You're absolutely sure about this, Barney?"

"No doubt about it. When we have a sample this large to work with, it's pretty impossible to make an error."

Megan nodded. "Thanks for calling. I appreciate it." She pushed the End button and disconnected the line.

Bonnie and Tommy still weren't paying any attention to her, and she was glad for it. She would in time, of course, have to share this dreadful news with Bonnie, but not now. Not while Tommy was here. He had enough to handle without knowing that the dad who had kidnapped him had also tried to kill him.

"Will you two excuse me for a moment?" Megan decided to blaze a trail through the crowd so she could check in with the judge's clerk. She was starting to make some progress when her feet suddenly disappeared out from under her.

She slammed down on the floor hard, briefcase first. "What the —"

Twisting her neck around, she saw nothing behind her except a boy, maybe ten or so, who was working a little too hard at not looking in her direction.

"Did you trip me?" Megan said in a voice more than sufficient to turn many heads, including the boy's mother's.

The kid continued to look away, suddenly very interested in the dot pattern in the ceiling panels.

"Don't pretend you didn't hear me." Megan pushed herself to her feet. "Did you trip me?"

The boy's mother, a large woman who seemed plenty stressed out already without taking on any additional problems, intervened. "I'm sure it was just an accident. There are so many people crowded into this tiny room."

"If it was an accident, let him tell me so." She placed her hand on the boy's jaw and turned his head to face her. "How about it, kemo sabe? You think it's funny to trip people?"

The boy affected a pained expression. "Mommy, she's hurting me."

The mother slapped Megan's hand away. "Leave him alone!"

Megan was outraged. She wasn't entirely sure why, but after all she had been through today, she didn't need this. "Why are you defending him? He could kill someone like that."

"You're overreacting."

"I don't think I am."

"Leave us alone!"

"Your kid is a menace!"

The mother's voice was becoming fluttery and semi-hysterical. "I want you to leave us *alone!*"

"I want an apology."

"If you don't leave my son alone, I'll call the police!"

"Call away. I may decide to file charges for battery!"

"All right, all *right!*" The boy squirmed around in his seat. "I'm sorry," he said, under his breath. "I didn't mean it. Exactly."

"What, was it something I said? Something about my suit you didn't like?"

The boy shrugged. "Nah, I was just bored."

His mother patted the boy in a rough and rapid manner Megan suspected was not at all comforting. "We've been here since nine-thirty."

"And you haven't seen the judge yet?"

"Our lawyer hasn't shown up. He keeps calling, making excuses. So we're stuck waiting."

Megan rubbed her hand against her brow. Been in this hellhole since nine-thirty? No wonder the kid was stir-crazy.

"Look." Megan reached down to the bottom of her bag. "Ever seen one of these?" She pulled the ball-bearing contraption out and plopped it onto the kid's lap.

"No." He lifted one of the silver balls and let it crash down into the others, starting the chain reaction. "What does it do?"

"You're doing it already." Megan smiled at his mother. "Keep it. It may amuse him for a while."

"Oh, we couldn't possibly . . ."

"Please. I'll be glad to get it off my hands."

The mother reached for her own purse. "Then let me give you something."

"That really isn't necessary."

The mother withdrew a large glass bottle filled with green liquid. "I got this last night at the office Christmas party. You know, one of those gag gift exchanges."

Megan took the extra-large bottle of Listerine. "Boy, those gag gifts are some kind of funny, aren't they?"

"I gave a giant-size roll-on Arrid Extra Dry."

"That's clever, too." She dropped the mouthwash into her bag, which was now even heavier than before. "Well, thanks very much."

The mother smiled and waved. "Merry Christmas."

Megan waved back. "Ho, ho, ho."

As it turned out, once they got in, the hearing took less than ten minutes. Judge Harris, a middle-aged career judge who knew her way around domestic law backwards and forwards, was particularly expeditious, in part no doubt due to the size of the horde outside. The judge would probably be on duty till midnight no matter what she did.

Megan put Bonnie on the stand to give a brief account of her nightmarish life since her breakup, of how Carl had stalked her and her son, threatened her, even tried to poison Tommy. Then, in a broken voice, barely able to speak, she told the horrific account of Carl's visit to her home that morning, of punching her boyfriend and neighbor, of smashing his hand through the windowpane. Megan suspected Bonnie could've gotten her restraining order right then and there, but after Bonnie proceeded to recount Carl's attempt to kidnap Tommy, there was no uncertainty about the outcome.

Just for good measure, Megan entered into evidence a copy of the police reports for each of the earlier incidents. And in return, she got an impressive-looking restraining order signed by the judge, prohibiting Carl Cantrell from coming near Bonnie, Tommy, or their home.

"I'll schedule a formal hearing for three weeks from today," Judge Harris said, marking the date on her calendar. "You'll have to serve notice on her ex-husband before then."

"I'll take care of it, your honor," Megan said, making notes.

"Do you have any idea where the man is?"

"No. But I'm hoping the police will find him. They do have his license-plate number."

The judge nodded. "I hope so, too. For everybody's sake."

12

By the third round, Carl was drinking Scotch and water, hold the water. But the medicine was doing its work; the liquid comfort coursed through his veins, numbed his body. After a while he was able to forget the pain — the physical pain, at any rate. The only reminder came every time he bent his elbow, as the sharp stabbing agony reminded him that he had sliced up his arm only hours before.

He tossed back the remains of his shot glass, savoring the sensation of hot burning fluid hitting the back of his throat. Feel the burn, as the boys on the force used to say. Feel it washing away all the hurt, all the misery. It erased everything, Carl realized.

Everything except memory.

He couldn't forget that it was Christmas Eve. He couldn't forget that his son would be spending the day with some slimeball who wasn't his father. He couldn't forget that his wife would be spending the night with the same slimeball. And he couldn't forget that he had failed to do a damn thing about it.

"I'll haveanotherround," he said, marginally aloud. Was he slurring his words? Damn, he thought maybe he was. And maybe that was a good sign. He'd long since acquired the skill of drinking to excess and not letting the effects show. Maybe this meant he was crossing a new threshold, reaching a new peak.

Or maybe he was just becoming a sloppy drunk. Who the hell knew? Either way, he wanted another drink.

"Hey, Joe!" he shouted. "Hit me!"

The substantial, big-boned man with the white apron around his waist pivoted in Carl's direction. "My name ain't Joe."

"Ain't —" Carl slapped his forehead, a bit harder than he really intended. "Right, right. Joe tossed me." He attempted a grin that he hoped might be something like charming. "And your name is — ?"

"Mister Bartender to you. And I think you've had enough."

"Aw, don't start with that. I hate that." He could tell he was weaving a bit, which could be dangerous on a bar stool. He cleared his throat, concentrated on controlling his body movement and diction. "Come on, please. I'm just getting started."

"I could get my license yanked if —"

Carl spread his arms wide. "Hey, it's Christmas!"

Mister Bartender whipped a Scotch bottle out from beneath the counter, a bitter frown on his face. "This is the last one, buddy. And I mean it."

Carl scooped up the refilled glass and cradled it in his hands. "You're a Christian saint, pal. A Christian saint." The glass was mere inches from his lips when he heard a shrill beeping noise from somewhere nearby.

He jumped, almost spilling the precious contents of the glass. He focused his eyes, trying to stop the room from spinning. Was that some kind of fire alarm? Was there a raid?

He noticed that all the other patrons at the bar were looking at him. Did they know something?

The burly bearded man at the next stool leaned his way. "It's your phone, you mook."

He pressed his hands against his chest. Damn! His cell phone; he'd almost forgotten he had the thing. Not like anyone ever called anymore.

He whipped the phone out of his coat pocket. He hoped he had enough battery power to take the call; he couldn't remember the last time he'd charged it. 'Course, at the moment, he couldn't remember much of anything.

He flipped the lid open and pressed the Send button. He twisted away from his neighbor, finding some measure of privacy on the other edge of his bar stool. "Yeah?"

"Carl, is that you?"

Carl froze. His lips parted, but he didn't know what to say, couldn't think —

"Bonnie?" It was barely a whisper, as if he didn't dare risk shattering the dream by saying her name out loud. "Is that you?"

"It's me, baby. Can you talk?"

This can't be real, he thought to himself. This can't be happening. "I — I can talk."

"Carl, I'm so sorry about everything that's happened. I never meant for things to turn out like this."

"I — I didn't either, honey."

"We shouldn't be fighting. A family should be together on Christmas Eve."

Carl's head was swimming, supercharged with adrenaline and excitement. "I know, honey. That's what I've been saying. That's what I've been saying all along."

"I've been so wrong, Carl. I've been so bad. I know I have."

"No, honey. It was me. All me."

"No, I've treated you like hell. I've kept you away from your boy. That was wrong. A boy needs his daddy."

Tears cascaded down Carl's cheeks. He couldn't help himself. She was saying all the right words. "It's okay, honey."

"It's not okay. It was wrong. But I'd like to make it better now. I mean — if you'll let me." He could hear her breathing deeply, swallowing her pride. "If you'll still have me."

"Of course I will, honey. You know I will."

"You're so good to me, Carl. You always have been."

"Aw, honey, I love you. You know I do."

"I know, Carl. I want you to come to me. Please. Now."

"But —" He pulled the phone away from his ear and stared at it. Was this a dream or a hallucination? "But what about Frank?"

"Frank is gone, Carl. Gone forever. He's out of my life."

"Are — are you sure, honey?"

"I'm sure. That was such a mistake. I don't know what came over me. But I know this: I want to start doing things right. Starting today. Starting with you."

"I do too, baby. I do too."

"And — oh, there's so much more I want to tell you. To show you. I'll — well, I'll let it be my Christmas surprise."

"I love surprises, baby. Especially from you."

"Please come to me, Carl. Come now."

Carl's hand began trembling. "I — I'll be right over, sweetheart. Where are you?"

"I'm at home. Don't ring the bell; I don't want Tommy to know that we're together again yet. Let it be his Christmas surprise. He'll be so happy."

"Whatever you want, Bonnie."

"Just come to the house and wait outside. When I see you, I'll come out to meet you."

"I'll be there, Bonnie. I'm leaving right now."

"Please do, Carl. I can't wait to be with you. I can't wait to hold you in my arms, to feel you pressing up against me —"

"I'm coming, Bonnie. I'm coming right now."

"And Carl?"

He jerked his head back to the receiver. "Yes, baby?"

"I love you, Carl. I — I always did, you know."

The line disconnected. Carl suddenly re-alized his face was bathed in tears. He was blubbering like a baby. Everyone in the bar was staring at him — and he didn't care. He just didn't care.

It would take him ten minutes to get back to the alley where he'd ditched the pickup. Maybe less if he ran. After that, it wouldn't take him fifteen minutes to get to Bonnie's house.

To *their* house.

He tossed the contents of his wallet down on the counter, wiped his eyes, and raced out the door. The bracing wind gripped him, shook him, roused him, cleared his head.

This was really happening, he told him-self. Really, really happening. He was coming home.

He was part of a family again. On Christmas Eve.

Bonnie stretched across the sofa and punched the button disconnecting the speakerphone. "How did I do?"

Frank sat at the end of the sofa, her feet in his lap. "You were brilliant. Absolutely brilliant." He bent down and kissed her big toe. "Do you think he'll come?"

She laughed. "I know he'll come." She

readjusted the pillow under her head. "Idiot."

"Good. And all will go as planned?"

"Are you kidding? The stage is set. After that scene you provoked this morning, after the fool tried to kidnap Tommy — hell, by now the police must assume he tried to poison the kid. They're scouring the city for him, and I've got a restraining order in my pocket — which the chump is about to violate. Everything is set up perfectly."

"I'm so glad." Frank wriggled the top of her foot into his mouth and nibbled on the tips of her toes.

"Will you be ready?" Bonnie asked pointedly.

"Oh, yes. Oh, yes." He lowered her feet gently to the sofa, then reached across the end table to his black tote bag. Carefully he removed the sturdy wooden box inside, opened it, and took out the shiny silver pistol resting inside.

He checked to make sure it was loaded. "Very ready."

Bonnie stretched out, her face settling into a happy smile. "That's good," she said, curling up like a kitten on the overstuffed cushions. "After all, I did promise the man a Christmas surprise." She began to laugh. "And boy, is he ever going to get one."

13

Carl was practically driving on autopilot as he made his way to Bonnie's house. The sky could've fallen down around him; he would never have noticed. All he could hear, all he could think about were those last tender words, the words that kept ringing in his ears and wouldn't stop: "I love you, Carl. I always did."

He had known she loved him, he thought as he zipped by the state capitol on Lincoln Boulevard. He'd known it. Deep down, she couldn't have meant all those horrible accusations. It was just a brain fever or something, just an aberration. Now they would get back to how things were supposed to be.

He swerved around the corner of Fifteenth Street, almost lifting the pickup onto two wheels. He wasn't driving well, he knew that. He'd had too much to drink. Couldn't see straight and wasn't thinking clearly, either. But what could he do?

He had to get there. He had to get there. He had to get there.

The words rushed back to him, blocking out all distractions, all reason, all rational thought.

"I love you, Carl. I always did."

Megan had just about decided to call it a day. She unhooked Jasper's leash and prepared to haul him home for whatever Christmas they could look forward to when the phone rang.

"He's coming!" the voice on the phone said before Megan had a chance to say hello.

"Bonnie? Is this you?"

"He's coming! He's on his way!"

"Carl? Carl is coming?" She wrapped the leash back around her lamp. "Does he know about the restraining order?"

"He doesn't care. He says he's coming to take Tommy away. And he says he'll kill anyone who gets in his way."

"Call the police, Bonnie."

"They won't come —"

"Bonnie, you listen to me!" Megan put on her most authoritative voice. "Hang up the phone and call the police. They *will* come. You don't have time to mess around. Call now!"

"All right."

"I'll come, too. But you have to call the police. Tommy's life is in danger. And so is yours!"

Frank brushed his hand around Bonnie's face, stroking her ears, caressing her chin. "Have I mentioned lately that you're magnificent?"

"Not as often as you should." She pushed herself up off the pillows. "I am rather good, though, aren't I? That little tremor I get in my voice? That broken, halting quality."

"Positively brilliant. So what are we going to do now?"

Bonnie slipped her hands playfully under his shirt. She stroked his chest. "Like the woman said. I'm going to call the police."

Carl knew he was taking the curve off Fifteenth Street too fast, but he couldn't help himself — he wanted to be there so badly! The tires screeched; he left a lot of rubber on the pavement. He swerved to one side and careened into the curb. He whipped the steering wheel around, trying to jackknife the truck back onto the street, but he was too slow. His truck plowed into the corner stop sign before he had even seen it.

He hit the brake and the pickup ground to a halt. Holy mother of —

He checked himself, making sure he was still intact, making sure he hadn't done any additional damage to himself. Everything seemed to still be attached. Still here. Still alive —

The pickup, however, was trashed. Smoke was rising out of the hood.

Never mind. He didn't have time for that. He didn't have time for anything except Bonnie. Bonnie and Tommy. Bonnie and Tommy and Carl, together again.

He popped open the glove box and removed the small service revolver he still had after all these years. Surely he wouldn't need it, not after everything Bonnie had said. But he wasn't taking any chances. Not anymore.

He slid out of the pickup cab, landed on his feet. His neck ached. But it didn't matter. Just didn't matter.

He could walk from here. Or run. It was barely half a block. He jogged down the side of the street, leaving the wreck behind, ignoring the pain in his neck, his back, his arm. He had to get to her. Had to get there now.

As he approached, a neighbor stepped out of the house next door. Was it the same man he had flattened this morning? Carl wondered. He couldn't remember. A neighbor was a neighbor, right?

"Now, Carl, I can't let you go in there."

Carl, the man had called him — like he knew him or something. Maybe he did — Carl wasn't sure. His vision was blurred and he was having a hard time making out the lines of the man's face.

"Why don't you just leave those nice folks alone?"

He was a big man, this neighbor was, Carl noted. But he knew he could take him. He hadn't spent all that time at the academy learning exotic self-defense methods for nothing. The man was an obstacle, that's all. An obstacle between him and his family. And he'd had about as much of those obstacles as he could take.

"Be reasonable, man. It's time to get on with your life."

Don't you see? That's what I'm *trying* to *do,* Carl thought, but somehow he couldn't make the words come out. It didn't matter. This was no time for words.

Carl reared back his fist and aimed a

roundhouse punch at the neighbor's chin. The man ducked, managing to avoid the swing.

"Don't make me hurt you, Carl. It's Christmas Eve. I don't wanna —"

"I will not let you keep me from my family!" Carl bellowed, then charged, gun at the ready. The neighbor turned and ran, looking as if he'd stared Death straight in the eye.

Once he'd chased the man out of the yard, Carl turned back toward the house, propelled by his confusion and rage. "I will not let you keep me from my family!" he shouted, waving his gun in the air.

"Not anyone. *Not anymore!*"

Inside the house, Frank and Bonnie crouched beneath the front window.

Frank tossed the pistol absently from one hand to the other. "Is it time?"

Bonnie smiled, then stroked him affectionately. "Not quite yet."

Megan pushed her car to the limit. She could hear the frame of the old rattletrap Toyota vibrating ominously, but she put it out of her mind. She blitzed down Lincoln Boulevard as quickly as she could, blazing a trail to Bonnie's house.

As she turned onto Fifteenth, she saw two black-and-white police cars making the same turn just ahead of her. Thank God — the word had gotten through. If Carl was desperate enough to violate the restraining order, to return to the house only hours after that scene this morning, he must've lost control, must've lost all grip on reality. There was no telling what he might do.

She pushed her little car down the seemingly endless length of Fifteenth Street, just praying that she and the cops got there in time.

Even in the midst of his rage, Carl remembered that she had told him not to come to the door. Wait outside, she had said. I want to surprise Tommy.

Well, here he was. He had fought like a maniac to get here. So where was she?

"Bonnie!" he cried out, but there was no response. "Bonnie!"

He couldn't bear to wait any longer. He ran up to the front door and began pounding.

"Bonnie!" he shouted, battering the door already splintered by his assault this morning. "Bonnie, I'm here! I'm ready!"

There was still no response. Carl could

feel sweat breaking out all over his body, chilling him. He didn't know how or why, but he had the distinct feeling that his most cherished dream was falling apart before it had ever really begun.

"Bonnie!" he cried. He started moving toward the window when he heard police cars making a beeline down the street. The shrill sirens raised the short hairs on the back of his neck. He knew if they saw him, they'd haul him away. He didn't have much time.

"Bonnie! *Please!*" Why didn't she open the door? He couldn't understand it. He knew she wanted him; she'd told him so. There must be something wrong, some horrible misunderstanding.

The first police car door opened.

"I just want to be with my family!" Carl cried out. His voice dripped with confusion and anguish. "I just want to be with my boy on Christmas Eve!"

"Don't do anything stupid," one of the cops said, his voice transformed into a metallic squawk by the electric bullhorn. "Drop the gun."

"No!"

"You can't win. We have you surrounded. You cannot escape. And we will not let you enter that house."

Carl glanced over his shoulder. The cops were out of their cars, three of them now. The doors were out and the officers were crouched behind them, primed and ready to shoot.

He could think of only one thing to do, one last chance. He knew the front bay window was weakened; he'd put his arm through it only this morning. If he hit it at top speed . . .

"I'm coming, Bonnie!" He crouched down in a sprinter's start and flew toward the broken window. He was barely five feet away when a chorus of shots rang out.

Carl stopped in his tracks. He froze up, twitching like a man having a seizure. And then he fell, like a man with no legs, tumbling into a heap on the yellow grass.

14

Still peering through the window, Bonnie couldn't help but express her amazement. "Nice shooting."

Frank caressed the hot barrel of his gun. "I aim to please," he said. "If you'll pardon the pun."

Bonnie grinned, then turned her eyes back out toward the front yard. "Next time the cops fire — finish him."

Megan screeched to a stop just as the shots rang out. No! she thought. I'm too late. I've failed her.

She jumped out of the car and ran toward the line of police cars barricading the street. "What's happening?" she asked, breathless, as she ran up behind them. "Are Bonnie and Tommy all right?"

"Stay back, lady," one of them growled.

Megan took one look and screamed. "Bonnie!" Ignoring the police, she ran forward, making a beeline for the front door of the house.

"Lady!" one of the cops barked, but Megan kept running. She could see now that Carl was lying in a bloody heap on the grass; she didn't see how he could possibly do her any harm.

She stopped when she reached the body, then groped stupidly for a pulse.

He was still alive.

"Where the hell did she come from?" Frank growled, lowering his gun. "Who is she?"

"It's the lawyer!" Bonnie answered. "Damn!" She had expected Megan to come, but not so soon, not spoiling everything.

"I can't tell if he's dead!" Frank spat the words out.

Bonnie whirled around, livid. "I know that, idiot."

"What are we going to do now?" He grabbed her by the arms and shook her. "Tell me that, will you? What are we going to do now?"

Bonnie broke out of his grasp, cursing under her breath. "I'll think of something."

"Call an ambulance!" Megan cried. The

three cops were moving her way, but one of them ran back to radio for the medics.

Megan stood up, raced toward the window. "Bonnie? Are you in there? Are you all right?"

A few moments later, the front door cracked open. "Megan?" a subdued voice whispered.

"Bonnie!" Megan ran toward the front door. They fell into each other's arms at the halfway point.

"Oh, Megan!" Bonnie sobbed. Her face was streaked with tears; her voice was trembling. "I — I was so frightened."

Megan led her back to sit on the front steps. "What happened?"

Several seconds passed as Bonnie tried to collect herself. "I was so scared. Even worse than before." She cradled her knees and hugged them close to her. "So scared."

"What did he do?"

She was breathing in short, broken gasps. "He just showed up, shouting and threatening. Said he was going to kill me. Said he was going to kill us all."

"What did you do?"

"I called the police, like you said. Thank God they got here quickly. He was crazy, Megan, just crazy. He tried to throw himself through the bay window."

Megan took Bonnie's head in her lap and held her tight. "It's all right, Bonnie. It's going to be all right. It's all over now."

"I — I just wish it hadn't had to happen like this," she said, sorrow tinging every syllable. "Poor Carl. What a way to go."

"Don't worry, Bonnie. He isn't dead."

Bonnie's eyes seemed to contract. "He . . . isn't?"

"No. The bullet hit him in the arm. Hurts like hell, I'm sure, but it isn't life-threatening."

"You're — sure?"

"Positive. I doubt if he'll be in the hospital overnight."

"Oh, Megan." She turned her head away. "I can't tell you what a relief it is to hear that."

"The important thing is, he's in custody. And after this stunt, he's likely to stay that way for a good long time."

She saw over her shoulder that the police were approaching. They would doubtless have questions of their own. "Bonnie, the police are going to need all the details. Do you want me to stay?"

"Do I need an attorney?"

"Probably not. But I thought you might need . . . a friend."

"Oh, that would be — you must have plans."

"Outside of feeding the dog, no."

Bonnie hugged Megan close to her. "You're so good, Megan. So good to me."

"Nonsense." Megan stood up and prepared to meet the police. "Least I can do. Especially on Christmas Eve."

15

More than two hours passed before Bonnie finally saw the last of the police, the medics, the family counselors. Carl was hauled off to St. Anthony's, Bonnie provided a detailed statement, and Frank remained in the upper bedroom, out of sight.

When finally she had cleared the last of the do-gooders out of the house, Bonnie made her way upstairs. Frank was smoking and watching some abysmal Christmas special, something involving talking animals and snowmen and, of course, Santa Claus.

"All gone?" Frank asked, stubbing his cigarette out in a cup.

"For now," Bonnie answered. She threw herself across the bed. "They'll be back day after tomorrow. And I'm supposed to go in and fill out some forms. File a formal complaint."

"I've got a few complaints myself," he

said, drawing a line with his finger down the curve of her neck, across the soft curve of her shoulders. "And Carl?"

"He's fine, more or less." Her voice acquired an edge. "You got him in the arm, and only barely that. Just a flesh wound, as they say in the westerns. It was the shock that made him collapse, not the wound."

"You're joking."

" 'Fraid not, lover boy." She rolled over to face him. " 'Course, the police are planning to arrest him as soon as he's able to move. They're going to charge him with assault and battery, resisting arrest, violating a restraining order. He'll do some time, no doubt about it."

Frank's teeth ground tightly together. "That isn't good enough."

"I'm aware of that, Frank."

"Jail time gets us nothing. He has to die."

"I'm aware of that, too, Frank. Are you blaming me?"

"It was your plan."

"It was your hand on the gun!" She sat upright. "You told me you could shoot!"

"I can shoot."

"Meaning, I guess, that you can pull a trigger. But you couldn't hit a man barely six feet away."

"For your information, it's hard to hit a moving target."

"He was moving toward you, Frank. Tommy could've hit him."

"Then maybe you ought to let him!" His voice swelled. "You can't leave him at his friend's house forever, Mommie Dearest. Why don't you pick him up and ask if he'd like to shoot his father for you? Since you don't have the balls to do it yourself!"

"Frank, don't be angry —"

"I don't know what's wrong with you! The man has to die, or this was all for nothing."

"Frank —"

"Sometimes I can't tell what you want."

"I want to be with you, Frank. I want what you want."

"That's not how it sounded to me."

Bonnie closed her eyes and swallowed. She had miscalculated, she realized, had pushed him too far. Now she was in danger of losing him. And she couldn't allow that to happen. She still needed him. "Frank, please calm down. I'm sorry. I didn't mean —"

"Didn't mean what?"

She laid her hands gently on his shoulders and began softly kissing his neck. "I didn't mean to blame you," she said between kisses. She knew she had to retreat, stroke him, bring him back to the game plan. "It's just so difficult. You know how much I lust after you."

"Yeah, right," Frank replied, but his voice was softening. "Me and the three million bucks."

"It's you I want," she said, using her most seductive voice. "I want you right now."

"Don't be ridiculous," Frank said, but he didn't push her away. "We have work to do. When do you think Carl will be out of the hospital?"

"Soon." She continued kissing, making her way to his head, nibbling his earlobe. "Like I said, the injury was minor."

"But as soon as he's discharged, the police will lock him away. And then we'll never be able to get to him. Unless we can figure out some way for him to escape."

"Escape?" she whispered, blowing gently into his ear. "Is that wise?"

"It's the only chance we have. If they get him back into custody, we have no chance."

"I see." She was snuggling closer, pressing herself up against him. "You're so smart, Frank. So damn smart."

"Once he's free, we can lure him back to

the house and finish what we started this afternoon."

"Is that possible?" She wrapped her right leg around him and squeezed. "He may be a drunk, but he isn't stupid. He'll never come back here after what happened today. No matter what crock I feed him over the telephone."

"He probably won't come back for you, true." Frank's hands were beginning to move, smoothing the curves of her body, searching for his favorite soft spots. "But you're not the only ace in the hole we have with that idiot. He'll come. And as soon as he does —" He raised his voice and adopted a near dead-on facsimile of Bonnie's voice. "I didn't know what to do, Officer. He was acting crazy, threatening me, hurting the boy. I had to shoot."

"Hey, that's pretty good," Bonnie said. "I had no idea you were so talented."

"Darling, you haven't even scratched my surface yet."

"But even if you do manage to set Carl up, won't everyone else be suspicious? The neighbors, the police? If he comes here again, even the cops might begin to suspect a frame."

"Not if they see him beating the kid."

"But Carl? He would never —"

"Trust me, dear. I can arrange everything."

"You are so bad." She pressed herself forward, jerking his shirt free of his pants, unfastening the buttons. "And you're so sexy when you're bad."

Frank smiled, wrapped his arms around her, and rolled her over. A moment later their minds were on a different subject altogether.

16

"Look, lady, if you're not his wife or kid or close relative, you're not getting in to see him."

"But it's very important."

"There are cops on duty."

"I've spoken to them. They said if I could get your okay, they'd let me in."

"But you don't have my okay."

"I know. That's why I'm here."

Megan pressed her hand against her brow. She hated bureaucracy. There was nothing worse. She had always thought that courthouse protocol was the most abysmal, but she was beginning to alter her opinion in favor of hospitals.

For fifteen minutes now, she'd been trying to get in to see Carl Cantrell, but she'd come smack-dab up against the Iron Maiden of nurse-receptionists. Normally she tried to stay as far away from child-napping poisoners as possible, especially when they were on the other side of a case. But she had business reasons for wanting to get in there. It wouldn't take long. It would be over in minutes. If she could just get Nurse Ratched here to give her the thumbs up.

"Look," Megan implored, "this is critical. A woman's life may be in danger. And that of her son."

"Because you can't get in to see a patient? I don't think so, honey."

Megan drew herself up. "I want to take this up with your superior."

"Good luck finding my superior. Or my inferior, either. Lady, do you not understand that this is Christmas Eve?"

"I don't see what —"

"Most people are at home with their families. We're on a skeleton staff here, barely enough people to keep the place running."

"Nonetheless —"

"I've been on duty since four a.m., and won't get to go home until midnight. I've had no relief, no coffee breaks. No chance to lie down and take a nap. I haven't even had a chance to brush my teeth. My breath smells like death warmed over —"

"Lucky I happened by." Megan opened her shoulder bag and rummaged around until she found the bottle of mouthwash she'd gotten from the woman at the courthouse. "Duck into the bathroom and have yourself a gargle."

"You carry jumbo-size mouthwash in your purse?" Her eyes narrowed. "What are you, some kind of bag lady?"

"It was a Christmas present."

"Some friends you got."

"It was — you know — a joke. From an office party."

"Oh, right." Her stern exterior softened a bit. "I got one of those, too." She reached down to the shelf beneath her station, then plopped a hardcover book onto the counter. "This was mine."

Megan read the dust jacket. *How to Catch and Keep the Mate of Your Dreams.* "Well, that was very . . . thoughtful."

"Yeah, right. A friendly commentary on my winning personality." She grasped the big green bottle. "I'll tell you what. I'll take the mouthwash. You keep the book."

"Deal," Megan said, looking up expectantly. "And . . ."

"I suppose it'll be all right if you go in there. But don't stay too long. I don't wanna get in trouble."

"Understood. I'll be brief."

The nurse raised the mouthwash bottle

and made a little salute. "Merry Christmas."

Megan smiled back. "Ho, ho, ho."

After the receptionist gave them the high sign, the two cops on duty outside the hospital room waved Megan through.

He was sitting upright in bed, eyes open wide. Megan was startled. She halted, staring at him. Somehow, in her mind's eye she had imagined he would be sleeping or drugged or hooked up to a million tubes or otherwise incapacitated. Instead, he looked little different from when she had seen him in the restaurant, except that his right arm was bandaged and in a sling. Nonetheless, he looked as if he might leap out at her at any moment.

Megan felt her mouth go dry. In her days as a priest, she had been forced to spend time with all kinds of unsavory characters. But she couldn't think of an instance when she'd been this close to a killer. This close to someone who had cold-bloodedly tried to murder his own son.

"You were at The Snow Pea," Carl said, breaking the silence.

"That's right. I was."

"Who are you, anyway?" His lips curled a bit. "One of Bonnie's friends, I suppose."

"That's, um, right." Megan cleared her throat. "Actually, I'm her attorney."

"You're not the chump who got her divorced."

"No, I'm . . . new."

"Wonderful. And to what do I owe the honor of this visit?"

Megan wished she had a glass of water. Her throat was so parched she could barely speak. "I'm glad to hear you're going to be all right. They told me the bullet didn't do any permanent damage. That the previous wound to your arm did more damage than the bullet."

"Your concern is touching, but if you're here on some obnoxious errand for Bonnie, I'd just as soon you got it over with."

"As you wish." Megan edged forward, just close enough that she could touch the edge of the bed, then pulled two thrice-folded documents out of her purse. "This is a copy of the restraining order that was issued today by Judge Harris. It orders you to stay away from your wife, your son, and their home."

"Ain't that swell. Anything else?"

"Yes." She tossed the other document on his bed. "This is to serve notice on you that a hearing has been set for the fifteenth day of January next year, at which time the judge will decide whether to make the order permanent. You can read the details in the notice. I must tell you, though, that if you decide not to attend the hearing, in all probability the order will be granted by default."

"Thanks so much." He stared down at the papers on the bed, but didn't touch either of them.

Megan was puzzled. He seemed bitter, yes, but he was not hostile or belligerent. There was nothing threatening or evil about him. She realized that in the perhaps one minute she'd been in the room with him, her fear had melted away and been replaced by a different sentiment altogether.

She was feeling sorry for him.

"Carl, how — how did this mess get started?"

"Meaning what?"

"Meaning . . . I don't know. The threats. The fighting. All this unhappiness."

Carl looked away. "Why do you want to know? Is this some trick to improve Bonnie's case against me?"

"No. It's nothing to do with that. I just . . ." Her voice faded. "I don't know. I was just curious. And I thought you might

132

like to talk to someone."

"Even if I did, it wouldn't be you. You don't strike me as the listening type."

"Really?" Megan couldn't explain why, but for some reason she wanted to understand this man. Something about the whole situation was beginning to trouble her. "I used to spend most of my time listening. People seemed to think I was pretty good at it."

"Why on earth would you want to listen to people? Were you getting paid by the hour?"

"This was before I was a lawyer. I was a priest."

"A —" He turned his head and did a double take. "A priest? But you're —"

"Yes?"

Carl's voice dropped a notch. "You're a woman."

"Thanks!"

"I mean, I didn't know there were female priests. 'Cept maybe in China or something."

Megan bit back her grin. "You've been away from church too long, Carl. The Episcopal church has ordained female priests for a good many years now. I wasn't even one of the first."

"Wow. Sorry, my parents were Southern

Baptists. I didn't know." He looked up at her again. "And does that mean —"

Megan had seen the look before; she knew where the conversation was going. "Episcopal priests are allowed to marry."

"Really?" For the moment, at least, he seemed to have forgotten his own problems. "So when'd you give up being a priest?"

Megan's eyes darkened. "April 19, 1995." She smoothed a wrinkle in her skirt. "Oh, I didn't stop that very day. But that's when it was all over for me. That's when I lost my faith."

"That's the day the Murrah building was bombed, isn't it?"

Megan nodded grimly. "My mother was in the building, working in the Social Security office. She was trapped in the wreckage for hours, bleeding, in pain. Listening to the agonized cries of her friends. She survived, but then again, not really." Her head dropped. "She was never the same."

"And you stopped being a priest after that?"

"It's hard to explain. I mean, it sounds so trite in a way. I certainly wasn't a stranger to tragedy. I saw it every day as a priest. I saw it happen to other people, that

134

is. But never to me." She brushed her hair back, looked away. "Mother recovered her strength, but not her spirit."

"Where were you when the bomb exploded?"

"At St. Paul's. That's where I worked. The cathedral is a block away from the Murrah building, but it was still ruined. All that beautiful stained glass — shattered. A shining testament to faith destroyed. In the blink of an eye." She rubbed her face furiously. "And all because some poorly educated zealots — some supposed Christians with an axe to grind — decided they had the right to ruin hundreds of lives." She bit down on her lower lip. "Well, if something like that could happen . . . it was very difficult for me to believe there really was a God. Or if there was a God, and he would allow that to happen . . . well, then I didn't want to be one of his priests."

Carl stared at the floor. "My mom died. Almost ten years now." He lifted his head. "You still miss her?"

Megan's eyes met his. "Every day."

"That's what it's all about, isn't it? That's why you lost faith. Your mother is gone, but you haven't really let her go yet. And you haven't forgiven God for what happened to her." His tone changed. "So you went to law school?"

"Why not? I still wanted to help people. But for real this time, not in a mushy-squishy spiritual way. I wanted to get down in the trenches and fight. Help the wronged find justice. Stop deadbeat dads. Protect women from abusive — um, well, you know."

Carl frowned. "Yeah, I know."

"I made great grades in law school, and next thing I knew, I was being courted by all these big law firms — Crowe Dunlevy, McAfee Taft. They seemed very supportive of what I wanted to do. So I took my best offer and joined a big corporate firm. How could I resist?"

"Except it didn't turn out the way you expected."

"No, it didn't." She fell silent.

"Maybe you ought to quit the firm. Set up your own shop."

Megan sighed. "That would be wonderful. But it would require tons of start-up capital, which I don't have. And even if I did . . ." Her eyes drifted. "I'm not sure I could bring it off." She looked up abruptly. "I don't know why I'm telling you this. It isn't why I came."

"Don't apologize," he said. He shifted

around in the bedsheets, as if he wanted to move but had nowhere to go. "Bonnie tell you what happened to me?"

"No. I mean, she said you used to be a cop. And that you . . . um . . ."

"Liked to drink? Except I bet that's not how she put it."

Megan almost smiled. "Well, no. It isn't." She inched forward. She couldn't explain why, but suddenly she was interested in hearing more of his story, knowing more about what brought him where he was today. "Tell me what happened."

Carl shrugged, looked away. "It was a while back, just a few months before the bombing, actually. Me and my partner got into some trouble. A shoot-out. Gang warfare. Near downtown. Bullets were flying. We were on our own for almost half an hour before reinforcements arrived."

"That must've been a nightmare."

He shrugged again. "We pulled through. But one of the gang members didn't. He got shot dead."

Megan's hand covered her mouth. "I remember reading about that."

"At first the reporters were our buddies. Talked about how heroic we were. The thin blue line holding back the mongrel hordes."

"But that didn't last."

"Two days after the shooting, the word broke. The kid that got killed — he was only thirteen." Carl swore under his breath. "Big for his age. And he was packing. But that didn't change the public reaction. We'd killed a thirteen-year-old kid. And two days later, ballistics dropped the final straw." His face seemed to tighten. "The bullet that killed the kid came from my gun."

Megan's lips parted. "That must've been horrible."

"Needless to say, the press were no longer my buddies. They demanded an investigation. How could this happen? Where did procedures break down? And pretty soon you're hearing words like *trigger-happy*. And *baby-killer*."

Megan laid her hand on the rail of his bed. "And that's when you began to drink?"

"Aw, I'd always had a drink or two on occasion. But that's when it turned ugly. That's when it became like the only thing I wanted to do in life was have another drink." He pounded his pillow. "Internal Affairs did an investigation, then cleared me. One hundred percent without blame. Acting in self-defense. But it didn't matter.

The paper didn't carry that story, natch. The big bosses decided it would be best if I laid low, took a desk job. Which I was horrible at. Hell — if I'd wanted a desk job, I'da become an accountant. I kept drinking and my work was crap and eventually they put me on extended leave. Without pay."

"And you kept on drinking."

"Like you wouldn't believe." His lips were thin and pursed. "I — I don't know how to explain it. I just stopped believing in everything I had believed before, everything I thought was right. It's like you were saying — I just lost faith. You know what I mean?"

Megan nodded. She certainly did. "Maybe if you had more faith in yourself, you wouldn't need the bottle."

"Maybe so. I kept thinking that Bonnie would come around. That she'd support me. Help a little, you know?"

"And she didn't?"

"Hell no. I came home one night, found her rolling on the kitchen floor with this creep Frank. They were going at it hot and heavy."

"Before you were divorced?"

"Months before. Before she'd even filed. And I'll tell you something else." He leaned closer. "Tommy was in the house. And awake. Now that's sick, if you ask me."

Megan tried to recall her first conversation with Bonnie that morning. Hadn't she said that she didn't start with Frank until after the divorce? "That must've been . . . very disheartening."

"That's one way to put it, yeah."

"But Carl — even with all that happened — why the turmoil? Why the violence?"

"Violence? What violence?"

"Bonnie told me you pummeled Frank in the face this morning."

"Do you know what he was saying? He was taunting me, telling me how he was doing . . . horrible things to my boy. Said he was going inside to do it again right then."

"So you —"

"Yes! What else could I do? Stand still and let him torture my boy?"

"He couldn't have meant it."

"Then why would he say it?" Carl pressed his hand against his forehead. "It was crazy. Almost like he wanted me to hit him."

His words struck a dissonant chord inside Megan's brain. Almost like . . . "I hear you took a swing at two of Bonnie's neighbors. This morning and this afternoon."

"They were trying to keep me from my son. I was desperate to see him. Desperate! It was Christmas, and I couldn't just leave him there with that pervert."

"So you snatched him."

"Of course I did. Wouldn't you?" He shook his head. "Never dreamed it would be so easy."

It *was* easy, Megan thought silently. After that incident in the morning, surely Bonnie could've foreseen . . .

"I'll admit, I was thinking about taking Tommy on the road. Holing up somewhere till I could get some help for myself, hire some lawyers, get custody for real."

"But, Carl, you tried to poison Tommy!"

"What are you talking about?"

"The Chinese food. It was poisoned."

"What?"

"And Bonnie told me you'd tried it once before."

Carl lurched forward abruptly and grabbed Megan's arms. "You have to listen to me. I would never hurt Tommy. Not in any way. Much less kill him."

"You put something on his food."

"I put soy sauce on his food! So what? I was trying to get him to eat it. I just — I just wanted us to have a happy moment together. One time when everything went the way it should. You have to believe me — sure, I was thinking about taking him away from his mother and that sick piece of work Frank. But I would never hurt Tommy. I would never do that!"

Megan looked deeply into the man's eyes. She almost hated to admit it to herself, but she did believe him. She really did.

"I know I've been acting crazy," Carl said. "Been that way all day. I don't know why. It's — it's something about the holiday. All this Christmas peace-on-earth-and-goodwill-toward-man stuff. Presents. Families getting together. Except me. I don't have anyone." His lips pressed together. "I used to love Christmas. Tommy and me — we both loved it. Back before the split. It was a truly special day." He laughed. "I have this ratty old Santa suit; he loved it when I dressed up in that thing. He knew it was really me, but — somehow it didn't matter, you know? We just —" His voice wavered; he stopped till he regained control. "We just had so much fun together."

Megan looked down quietly. "I'm sorry, Carl."

"All day I kept dreaming that eventually this nightmare would end. Bonnie would dump Frank, I'd get straightened out — we would be one happy family again. But it didn't happen." His jaw clenched. "I had to face facts. I'd been kidding myself since the day we were married. All along I'd been telling myself, Don't be so suspicious. It's you she loves. Really it is." He shook his head. "But it wasn't. It never was. It was the money."

Megan blinked. "The money?"

"You got it. Makes the world go round, right?"

"She married you for a cop's salary?"

Carl grinned. "Hardly. Naw, my dad was loaded. He was R. F. Cantrell, the construction magnate. You may have heard of him — built half of Oklahoma City. Left me three million bucks."

"Three million? But then — why were you —"

"I don't have it yet," he explained. "It's held in trust. Dad wanted to make sure the moolah didn't prevent me from making something of myself. Hell of a joke, huh? Right now, I barely get enough to live on. But when I hit forty, two years from now, I get it all."

Megan felt a gnawing sensation in the pit

of her stomach. "Carl, if something happens to you, who gets the money?"

Carl shrugged. "I'm not really sure. My heirs, I guess."

"Have you made a will?"

"A long time ago. Just after . . ." He paused. "After I got married."

"And who inherits? Under your will."

Carl's voice became distinctly quieter. "Bonnie does. She gets everything."

"And you didn't change your will? After your divorce?"

"No. I never thought about it. And of course deep down, even though I'd never admit it, I always hoped we'd get back together again. I think she does, too, deep down. She told me so on the phone. I wasn't hallucinating; she really said it. She told me how much . . ."

Carl went on, but Megan wasn't listening anymore. A dark thought had lodged in her brain, and now that it had established itself, she was having a hard time pushing it aside. It seemed incredible. But what if . . .

Megan rose out of her chair.

"Where are you going?" Carl asked.

"Police station," she murmured. "I want to do some checking."

"On what?"

"I'll tell you when I return." She started toward the door, then stopped. "Just promise me this. Promise you won't do anything foolish. Until I get back, just stay put and stay out of trouble, okay?"

"Well, I guess, but —"

"Please. I'll be back as soon as possible. And maybe, just maybe" — she headed out the door — "maybe this time I'll actually understand what's going on."

17

"Lady, I shouldn't even be talking to you."

"I'm sure that's true. But if you could just help me —"

"No. I'm sorry. Absolutely not."

"But I have to learn —"

"I said *no*."

Megan ran her hand through her thick black hair. Dealing with Barney Palmer, the man in toxicology, was proving more difficult than she had imagined. So far, he had been utterly unwilling to augment the information he had given her over the phone.

"But you're certain that the Chinese food was poisoned."

"I already told you that." Palmer was a paunchy man with sandy hair and a slightly receding hairline. He was maybe five or six years younger than Megan. "Sergeant Conner told me to advise you of that fact. But he didn't instruct me to tell you anything else."

"This could be of critical importance. Surely you've given out this sort of information in the past."

"Actually I haven't. This isn't really my job."

Her eyebrows rose. "It isn't?"

"No, I'm just filling in."

"What do you normally do?"

He appeared more than a bit miffed. "I'm the coroner. Didn't you know?"

Megan thought carefully before speaking. "Should I?"

"I've been on the evening news. Twice now." He made a minute adjustment to the lay of his tie. "Phil Coburn normally works toxicology, but he's off making merry, so they asked me to fill in. I guess they figured I already stank permanently of formaldehyde. A few more chemical odors couldn't do me any harm."

Megan tried to steer the conversation back to the topic. "I still need more information about this alleged poisoning —"

"Then fill out the forms. Get authorization from my boss."

"Your boss isn't in. It's Christmas Eve, remember?"

"How could I forget?" All at once Palmer slumped down into a chair. "It's Christmas Eve, and here I am all by myself, the only man on duty in forensics, the only soul so pathetic he's still at work."

This was a somewhat unexpected turn of events. "Drew the short straw, huh?"

"Hell no. I volunteered."

"Volunteered? To work Christmas Eve?"

He waved a hand in the air. "Not like I had anything better to do."

Megan's head tilted to one side. Now she was beginning to get the picture. "No holiday plans?"

"My family all lives in Europe, and I can't possibly afford to visit."

"No wife?"

"Not even a girlfriend." He let out a long sigh. "Look — you're a woman, right?"

"I think so."

"Then you tell me. What's my problem? Why can't I get a date?"

Megan suddenly felt flushed. "I don't know. Could it be . . . because you're a coroner?"

Barney's head dropped. "That's what I figured. And that's so unfair. There's nothing wrong with being a coroner. It's really a very sexy profession."

"I'm not sure I want to hear about this."

"I don't mean in that way, you sicko. I just mean it's exciting, glamorous. Working side by side with the detectives, solving crimes."

"You get to do that?"

"Not often." He winked. "But the women don't know that."

Megan suppressed a smile. "Barney, you're a very likeable person. I'm sure there's someone out there for you. If you just wait patiently, in time —"

"Oh, spare me the Father Knows Best speech. I'm hopeless. Whatever it is women like, I don't have it."

A lightbulb suddenly lit above Megan's head. "Barney, I may have something for you." After inspecting the contents of her shoulder bag, she pulled out the book she had gotten from the nurse-receptionist.

Barney read the cover. " 'How to Catch and Keep the Mate of Your Dreams.' " He looked up. "And you carry this around in your purse? Man, you must be worse off than I am."

Megan coughed. "Actually, it was a gift."

"Yeah, right." He thumbed through the pages. "Still, it can't do any harm. Mind if I hold on to this for a while?"

"No, please. Keep it. It's yours. Merry Christmas."

His eyes softened a bit. "Really? Hey,

thanks." He turned abruptly. "Here, let me get you something."

Megan held up her hands. "Don't bother. I —"

"No, I want to." He walked over to his desk and pulled a small object out of a box. "Here. You take this."

Megan held out her hands and received the gift. It appeared to be a small plastic reproduction of a school bus. "Gee, thanks."

"My sister sent it to me. Apparently it's all the rage in Europe."

Megan tried to imagine it — a tiny plastic bus was all the rage . . .

"It's a record player."

She looked up. "Beg your pardon?"

"A record player. See?" He flipped over the bus. "That's the needle on the underside. These holes on the sides are speakers. The wheels make it go around in a circle."

"But how —"

"You put it on top of a phonograph record, and as it drives around in a circle on top, the needle plays the music, which comes out the speakers. Ingenious, huh?"

"More like incredible."

"Sounds like hell, of course, and it destroys the record. But it's a great gimmick, don't you think?"

"Great isn't quite the word." She opened

her purse. "You're sure you want to part with this?"

He waved his hand. "Oh, yeah. It's a CD world now, right? I sold off all my LPs a long time ago."

"Swell." She dropped the bus in and closed her purse. "Well, if you're sure you can't help me . . ."

"Wait."

Megan stopped in her tracks.

"Look . . . I shouldn't do this . . ."

Megan listened intently, hoping for a *but*.

"But since you've been so nice, let me tell you something. There really wasn't much more we could determine. The food *was* poisoned. Rat poison, absolutely deadly."

"It must taste awful."

"Yes, but the taste would've been masked by the strong spices of the food."

"Tommy wouldn't have known it was poisoned."

"Probably not. If he'd taken more than a few bites, he'd have died almost instantly. We couldn't possibly have saved him."

Megan nodded her head grimly. Then Carl really was trying to —

"There was one interesting factor, though." He riffled through the papers on his desk, searching for the report. "Chemical analysis revealed a very low absorption rate."

"Low absorption rate," Megan repeated. "What does that mean?"

"It means the poison was still mostly topical. It had not soaked into the food."

Megan nodded her head. "Is that important?"

"Could be. We tested the food ourselves independently, with separate samples of poison we had here in the office. Toxin absorption didn't take long at all."

Megan was beginning to get the gist of the matter. "Then if the poison on Tommy's food hadn't soaked in much, even by the time you got it in the lab . . ."

Barney nodded his head. "Then it hadn't been there very long. One of the witnesses in the restaurant said their food had been delivered as much as twenty minutes before you arrived. There's no way the poison was applied that long ago."

"Then it must've been added later," Megan said, thinking aloud.

"Right," Barney confirmed. "It must have been added — well, not long before you arrived at the scene."

Megan nodded her head slowly. "Or after."

18

"Dinnertime, Mr. Cantrell."

Carl snapped out of his reverie. The painkillers had made him forget all about the pain in his arm. What occupied his thoughts now was that woman. That priest — or ex-priest or whatever. He had almost forgotten what it was like to actually talk to another human being, to be able to explain how you feel, to have the sense that the person on the other end was actually listening. She truly seemed to care; when she said she would check into the situation, he believed her.

The candystriper plopped the plastic tray across his lap, attaching the metal clamps on either end to the rail of his bed. "Looks like they've got something special for you tonight." She cast her eyes down toward the tray. "Red Jell-O with bananas and marshmallows. I love that stuff."

"You're welcome to mine," Carl growled.

The candystriper laughed. "Oh, what a card you are. But I doubt if the docs would approve of that. Or the two guards at the door."

"I'm surprised they let you in."

She opened his milk carton and poured it into a glass. "Everyone has to eat, Mr. Cantrell. Even when they're under guard."

"Did they taste it? To make sure I'm not being poisoned?"

The candystriper wagged her finger. "I get the impression they're more worried about what you might do than they are about what someone else might do to you." She smiled, then sauntered out the door.

Carl stared down at the plate. The effects of all the alcohol he had downed earlier had faded, but he still didn't have much appetite. Especially not for mystery meat. Or white milk. Or red Jell-O with bananas and marshmallows.

Well, he supposed he should eat something. He yanked the white napkin out from under the silverware.

A scrap of paper fluttered into his lap.

What's this? He recovered the scrap, frowning, and unfolded it.

It was a note. A Post-it note folded three times over.

The text was simple enough: BE READY

TO GO IN FIVE MINUTES.

Who was this from? he wondered, brow creased. The candystriper? Surely not. She must just be the courier — and probably an unwitting courier at that.

Bonnie? Tommy? Stop dreaming, he told himself. It was clear now that Bonnie wouldn't lift a finger to help him, and Tommy was too young to pull off something like this.

The lawyer-priest? She did say she would do some checking. He didn't expect anything like this . . . but it seemed the only possible explanation.

He glanced at his watch. At least a minute had passed since the candystriper left the room.

He scooted the tray away and climbed out of bed. He didn't know what was going on, but if he really was going to have a chance to get out of here, he didn't want to blow it.

He found his clothes draped over a hanger in the closet. They were in pretty bad shape, particularly the shirt, but at the moment, he couldn't afford to be choosy. He slipped out of the peekaboo hospital gown, crawled into his clothes, collected his cell phone, and waited.

He didn't have to wait long. A few minutes later, a huge explosion rocked the building. One moment he was leaning against the wall, and the next he was flying across the room, spiraling out of control.

Instinctively Carl gripped the bed. The floor shook violently, like someone had driven a semi into the foundations of the hospital. Everything that wasn't nailed down began to rattle and crash.

He staggered to the door and peered through the glass window in the center. Everyone outside had been caught off guard. People were reeling, falling. Thick files tumbled down, sending paper flying in all directions. Medicine bottles smashed down, hitting the tile floor and shattering into pieces.

"Not again!" one woman cried, and Carl knew immediately what she meant. Not again, not another bomb in Oklahoma City.

After a few seconds had passed, the trembling began to subside. Dust and smoke flooded into the waiting area, adding to the general confusion.

"Over there!" he heard the nurse-receptionist cry. She pointed toward an operating room in the back. "It came from over there!"

Carl saw the two guards outside hesitate,

glance at each other. They knew they were supposed to watch his door. At the same time they were the only authority figures in sight.

"In there!" the woman shrieked. "Hurry! I saw someone go in! There might be another bomb!"

A chorus of shouts and panicked cries punctuated her sentence. "Another bomb!" one of the interns cried. *"Run!"*

That made the decision for them. The two guards raced across the waiting area, plowing through the smoke to the operating room down the corridor.

Carl knew this was his chance. Making as little sound as possible, he pushed the pneumatic door open and slid through the opening. With all the confusion and smoke and dust in the air, no one noticed. He passed quickly by the elevator and headed for the stairs. Another couple of seconds and he was in the stairwell, moving down fast, but not too fast. As far as he could tell, no one had spotted him.

He hit the ground floor and broke into a sprint. He didn't really know what was going on, but he was smart enough to know he didn't have much time. This had been a gift — a Christmas gift, if you will — but it wouldn't last forever. Soon police and medics would be rushing to the scene of the explosion. And even sooner, those two guards would return to his room and see that he had hightailed it. When that happened, every cop in town would be looking for him.

He had to get back to his grungy apartment and collect a few things, before it got too hot. After that . . . well, he just didn't know. Until five minutes ago, he didn't think there was going to be an after that.

The brisk night air wrapped itself around him, invigorating him. He was glad to be out, to be free, but it didn't stop that one central question from nagging at him, tearing at his brain.

He couldn't kid himself — there was no way that lawyer-priest would set a bomb to bust him out of the hospital. So who did?

And more important — why?

19

When Frank came through the front door of the house, Bonnie was waiting with a perfect vodka martini, olive included. "Mission accomplished?"

Frank slid out of the thin white coat, took the drink, and downed it in a single gulp. He bit down on the olive, sliding the toothpick out between his teeth. "Mission accomplished."

"And you didn't have any trouble getting in?"

"Not the least." He flopped down on the sofa and propped his feet up on the hassock. "Once I put on the doc's coat and draped a stethoscope around my neck, everyone in the hospital started treating me like God."

She sat down, cuddling against him. "So did you get him out?"

"He got himself out. Where's my next martini?"

She jabbed him in the ribs. "Tell me!"

Frank grinned, then slid down lower on the sofa. "Slipped a note onto his food tray. Candystriper carried it in to him, never the wiser. Told him to get ready to run."

"And then?"

"Then I created a diversion."

She grabbed a pillow and beat him over the top of the head. "Will you stop making me beg for it? Tell!"

He grabbed her wrists and pulled her lengthwise across his lap. "I sparked an oxygen tank in one of the operating rooms. Created an explosion."

"No!"

"But I did."

"Was anyone hurt?"

"I sincerely doubt it. It was more show than substance. Made a huge noise, generated a ton of smoke. But I doubt if it did much real damage. What it did do, however, was allow your dear ex-husband to make his getaway."

She wrapped her arms around his neck. "You are so brilliant."

"I do my best."

"Where is he now?"

"How should I know? Probably crawled back to some bar. Doesn't matter."

"But we have to get in touch with him."

"Yes, darling, I know. But we don't want to be too speedy about it. Even an imbecile like him might think it a bit coincidental if —"

He stopped in mid-sentence. His head jerked around.

Tommy was crouched behind the banister. He was wearing Star Wars pajamas and clutching a teddy bear.

Bonnie whirled. "Tommy! What are you doing out of bed!"

Tommy had a miserable expression on his face. "I'm not sleepy."

She ran toward the stairs. "I don't care if you're sleepy or not! When I say get in bed, that means get in bed!"

Tommy took a step back. "Were you talking about Daddy?"

"You miserable brat!" Her hand whipped back and slapped him hard across the cheek.

"Ow!" Tommy squirmed away.

Bonnie grabbed him by the shoulders and shook him hard. "What did you hear, you sneak? *What did you hear?*"

"Nothin'," Tommy said. He twisted, unsuccessfully trying to get away. "I didn't hear nothin'!"

"Tell me!" Her hand reared back and

cracked him again across the face.

"I didn't!" Tommy began to cry. "I didn't!"

Frank came up behind them on the stairs. "There, there, now. Let's all get a grip on ourselves." He sat down between them and laid his hand gently on Tommy's knee. Tommy pushed it off. "Bonnie, if he'd heard anything, he would've told us, I'm sure."

"I didn't hear anything," Tommy repeated, choking.

"Of course you didn't. Your mother was just surprised to see you up again after she sent you to bed."

"I wasn't sleepy."

Bonnie leaned forward. "I don't care if you're —"

Frank gently pushed her back, silencing her. "Of course you're not sleepy," he said, maintaining the same even singsong voice. "Who would be? It's Christmas Eve. Tell you what. Are you hungry?"

Tommy shrugged. "A little."

"Well, then. Let's go get some food. A Christmas feast, I think. What's your favorite?"

Tommy glanced at his mother, then quickly looked away. "I like McDonald's, but Mommy says —"

"McDonald's it is, then. Happy Meals all around. After all, it's Christmas!" He patted Tommy on the shoulder. "Now you run upstairs and put your clothes back on. Get down here as soon as you can. We're going to party!"

Tommy wiped his nose, then wordlessly scrambled back up the stairs. A second later, they heard the door to his room close.

"And what was that all about?" Bonnie asked, hands on hips. "One minute you're a terrorist, the next you're Mr. Rogers."

Frank smiled thinly. "You weren't going to get any information out of him by beating him over the head. Didn't your mother ever tell you that you catch more flies with honey than vinegar?"

"My mother wasn't exactly the home-spun wisdom type. And our family wasn't exactly a 'Good night, John-Boy' bunch."

"Well, then let me take the lead. We have to gain the boy's trust. Eventually he'll tell us what he knows."

"And if he knows too much?"

Frank's eyes narrowed and darkened. "I'll leave that to your discretion." He glanced at his watch. "Speaking of family matters, I think it's time I called your ex." He started down the stairs. "Do you think he's still carrying his cordless?"

"I'm certain of it. He hasn't let the thing out of his sight since he got it."

"Good. That makes matters ever so much easier." He reached for the phone.

Bonnie placed her hand over his, stopping him. "Wait a minute. Let's think this thing through."

"We can't wait any longer. Your precious offspring will be down soon, ready for his french-fry fix."

"But I can't call Carl. Not now. And you can't either."

He lifted the phone. "I don't see why not."

"He'll recognize your voice."

"Don't be so sure. I'm a rather accomplished mimic, remember?"

"Frank, he got shot here, remember? Only hours ago. He may be a drunk, but he's not utterly brainless! He won't come here no matter what you say."

Frank turned to her, smiled, and said, in a near-perfect imitation of Tommy's high-pitched voice, "Please come, Daddy. Please. They're hurting me."

"You devil!" Bonnie's mouth turned up in a huge grin. "That's pretty good."

"More than good enough for cellular phone transmissions." He began to dial.

Bonnie came up behind him and wrapped her hands around his abdomen. "You're so bad," she purred, pressing up against him.

Frank smiled as he finished dialing the number. "I'm just getting started."

Carl stared at the whiskey bottle resting in the middle of the kitchen table in his one-room apartment. God, he wanted a drink. Wanted it so bad every cell in his body seemed to ache for it. Wanted it so bad his brain seemed to be ordering him to unscrew the lid and take a swallow.

But he kept thinking about what that damned busybody priest-lawyer had said. Her words kept coming back unbidden: Maybe if you had more faith in yourself, you wouldn't need the bottle.

Hell, what did she know anyway? It wasn't as if she had some hot line to the truth. It wasn't as if she'd been through what he'd been through.

He stared at that beautiful glistening damnable bottle. Just one drink would make him feel so much better . . .

But he wouldn't stop at one drink, of course. He wouldn't stop till he was lying on the floor swimming in his own urine, choking on his own vomit.

He turned away. He didn't have time for this now. The cops could show up at any moment. He'd deal with the bottle some other time, when he could think straight. Later. But not now.

He threw on his heavy coat, grabbed all the money and loose change he could find, and headed out the door.

He was almost gone when it called to him. Called him to come back.

Aren't you forgetting something? the bottle said.

He heard the sweet siren song ringing in his ears. It's me you really want, it sang to him. It's me you care for.

"It isn't true," he said aloud, teeth clenched. "It isn't."

When he heard the sudden shrill sound, he almost jumped out of his skin. "Cops," he murmured. "Gotta run." He was almost on the fire escape when he realized the ringing sound was coming from his coat pocket. His cell phone.

"Who could . . ." He didn't finish his question. There were only two possible answers. And they both seemed incredible.

He extended the antenna and pushed the Send button. "Hello?"

There was some static on the line, but not so much that he couldn't make out the words. "Daddy! Please come, Daddy!"

"Tommy?" He pressed the phone close against his ear. "Tommy? Is that you?"

More static. "Daddy, please! Help!"

"Tommy? Tommy, listen to me!" He felt torn apart, desperate. "Tommy?"

"He's hurting me, Daddy. He's hurting me real bad."

"Who is? Tommy? Can you hear me? Who's hurting you? Frank?"

The voice on the other end of the phone cried out in agony. "Please, Daddy. *Please!*"

Carl ran toward the door. "I'm coming, Tommy. Are you at home?"

"Yes, Daddy. And — can you wear the Santa suit? Like you used to."

Carl's brain raced. What had he done with the thing? Under the bed, in the closet . . . "I think so, son."

"Good. Wear the Santa suit, Daddy. Come to the back door — over the fence. So the neighbors won't see you."

Carl nodded. If one of those neighbors saw him now, they'd call the police in a heartbeat.

"Come at nine-thirty, Daddy. I'll sneak downstairs and meet you. You can come and take me away forever. Please!" The other end of the line clicked off.

Carl stood motionless, paralyzed with

horror. He didn't want to wait, he wanted to run out the door as quickly as he could.

But Tommy was right. If he just showed up like an idiot and got himself shot, he wouldn't do anyone any good. Least of all Tommy. And he couldn't call the police. They'd come after him, not Frank.

He ran back into the apartment. Like it or not, he would have to find that Santa suit and do as he was told.

He knew he was confused, knew he was probably screwing up somehow. But what could he do? His little boy was hurting. His little boy needed him!

He would have to go to him. Whatever the consequences.

20

Megan raced across the parking lot, shouting at the top of her lungs. "Mr. Collins! Mr. Collins!"

Mr. Collins, a balding middle-aged man with a salt-and-pepper mustache, stopped.

His hesitation gave Megan the chance she needed to catch up. She ran the rest of the distance, watching her breath circulate in the cold night air. It was getting colder; those predictions of snow seemed more likely by the minute.

She stopped just before she collided with the man. He stood patiently, hands in his trench coat, an eyebrow arched. "Something I can do for you, ma'am?"

She pressed her hand against her chest, trying to catch her breath. The night air stung in her throat. "You're the top man in ballistics, right?"

His brow wrinkled. "I suppose that's one way of putting it."

"That's what they told me at the front desk. Just before they closed up."

He nodded. "It is Christmas Eve."

"Believe me, I know." She took another deep breath. "What have you learned about the bullet that was fired at Carl Cantrell?"

He paused and scrutinized Megan with careful interest. "I don't think I recognize you. Are you on the police force?"

"Uh . . . no."

"D.A.'s office?"

"No."

"Member of the fourth estate?"

"No. But I took some journalism classes in college."

He did not appear amused. "Mind telling me why I would want to discuss the details of an ongoing investigation with you?"

"I'm a lawyer."

"Ah. Well, that makes everything perfectly clear." He turned and started toward his car.

"Wait." She ran forward, positioning herself between Collins and his Dodge. "I'm trying to find out as much as I can about what happened out there today. At the shooting. Before I arrived."

"Are you representing someone?"

"I represent Bonnie Cantrell. Or did, anyway."

"And she wants to know the results of the ballistics tests?"

"Well . . . no. Not exactly."

"Then I fail to see —"

"Look, I can't explain everything perfectly, okay? I haven't got it all figured out myself. I just have a really bad feeling about this, and sometimes, you have to trust your instincts and have faith —" She stopped, startled to find herself using the word. "I'm just afraid something terrible might happen if I don't get to the bottom of this."

"I'm sorry. I'm sure I would love nothing more than to help you . . . trust your instincts. But all investigations are confidential till the chief says otherwise."

"How do I get ahold of him?"

"On Christmas Eve? You don't." He pulled his keys out of his pocket and tried to gently nudge Megan out of the way.

"Wait!" she said, but he didn't. He popped open the driver's side door.

"But couldn't you just —"

"No! Now if you don't mind, I have some Christmas Eve plans of my own."

With the door open, the car interior was lit and Megan could make out the photo dangling on a string from the rearview mirror. "Is that your family?"

"Of course."

"I guess you're going home to them. For Christmas dinner."

He hesitated only a moment before answering. "Yes. Precisely."

"Lucky man." She inched forward. "Look, couldn't you just answer a few questions? You don't have to actually tell me anything. Just shake your head yes or no."

"I will not."

"Please!"

"I said no."

"It could be a matter of life or death."

"No!" For the first time, Collins's face began to flush red, and Megan didn't think the chill was the principal cause. "Please leave me alone!"

"I'll give you a present." Megan plunged her hand into the depths of her shoulder bag and came up with the treasure she had acquired in the toxicology lab. "See?"

Collins stared at the object in her hand. "You're offering me a plastic bus?"

"But it's more —"

"I didn't expect a million dollars, but as bribes go, that's pathetic."

"But it isn't a bribe. It's —"

"Yes?"

She drew in her breath. "It's a Christmas present."

"Ah. Well, that is different." Somewhat reluctantly he took the bus into his hands. "I suppose this is intended as a stocking stuffer for preschoolers?"

"Oh, no. Definitely for grown-ups. See, it plays records."

"What?"

"You heard right. There's a stylus on the bottom." She turned it over to show him. "You turn on the motor, put it on top of an LP, and it runs around playing the record. The sound comes out of those tiny speakers."

Collins drew in his breath. "What'll they think of next." He held it up to his face for a closer look. "Is the music quality good?"

Megan shook her head. "Sounds like hell, I understand."

"Is it good for your records?"

"Destroys them."

He shrugged. "Well, what was I going to do with them, anyway? Use them for Frisbees?" He slipped the bus into his pocket. "Okay, you made me an offer I can't refuse. Here, let me give you something."

"I promise you — that isn't necessary —"

He rooted around in the backseat of his

car, then emerged again. "The truth is, I lied to you."

"You did?"

"Yeah." His eyes clouded. "I'm not going to see my family. My wife and I are divorced. I get visitation, but she got Christmas. And she made it clear she doesn't want me anywhere near. I don't get to see my boy till New Year's." He looked at the wrapped package in his hands. "I bought this for my kid. Ordered it months ago. But if I know my ex-wife and her parents, by the time I see my boy next, he'll already have three of them. Why don't you take it?"

Megan held up her hands. "I really have no need —"

He pressed it into her hands. "You never know. Take it." Megan reluctantly accepted the gift. "So, anyway, what was it you wanted to know?"

Her eyes widened. "You mean you'll tell me?"

"Well, it is Christmas, after all. Almost. So you're investigating the Cantrell shooting?"

"Right." There was precipitation in the air, a bit too cold and dry to be rain. It was definitely going to snow. "Do you know who shot him?"

"No. And I'm not likely to find out through ballistics analysis, either."

"I thought every gun left individual markings on a bullet that could be used to trace it back to the gun that fired it."

"That's true. But the bullet has to be found in a condition such that it's possible to read those markings. This bullet was found lodged in the bark of a tree."

"Blast." Megan's fists clenched up. "I knew it passed through Carl's body, but I didn't know about the tree."

"I'm afraid the bullet was squashed on impact. The markings are absolutely unreadable at this point. For all I can tell, the bullet could have come out of any of a million guns."

"And there was nothing unusual about the caliber?"

"No. Exactly the same bullet all the city cops are firing."

Megan wrapped her arms around herself. All of a sudden she was feeling the cold. Even though she didn't know what it was, she had thought she was getting close to something. Now it seemed she had come up against a brick wall. "I had hoped I might learn something by talking to the police officer who actually shot him."

"Police officer? What do you mean?"

"I mean, if I could talk to the officer who fired the bullet —"

"Oh, no. There's no chance of that."

"I don't understand. You said the bullet was the same caliber —"

"And it is. But that doesn't mean he was shot by a cop."

"But . . . then who?"

"I can't tell you. But I can tell you this. I was with Barney when he inspected the wound and took pictures for the evidence file. The entry wound was in the forearm, in the front. The exit wound was in the back."

"I don't think I understand."

"I was given to understand the man was running toward the house when he was shot."

"That's true. He was."

"And I assume he wasn't running backwards."

"No, of course not."

"Then there's no doubt about it." He folded his arms firmly across his chest. "The bullet was fired from the house."

"What?"

"The police were behind him. They may have fired, but the bullet that hit the man came from in front of him. And that means it came from the house."

Megan grabbed his arm. "Have you told this to anyone yet?"

"Told who? Everyone's gone. It's Christmas Eve, for Pete's sake. I filed my report. And I expect the detectives working on the case will read it — when they get back after the holidays."

A sudden frisson of horror shot down Megan's spine. "That won't be soon enough." She spun around toward her car on the other side of the parking lot. "I have to tell Carl."

"Carl?" Collins called after her. "Carl Cantrell?"

"Right."

"Haven't you heard?"

Megan froze in her tracks. What *now?* "Heard what?"

"It was on the radio. Carl Cantrell broke out of protective custody. Eluded his guards and snuck away from the hospital where he was recuperating."

Megan's hands flew to her mouth. "Oh, no!"

"I'm afraid it's true. So you're not going to be able to tell him anything. Unless you know where he's going next."

The short hairs rose up on the back of Megan's neck. Something was bringing goose bumps to her skin, and it wasn't the cold. "I only hope I don't," she said, and without saying another word, she raced across the parking lot to her car.

21

Bonnie gazed into the mirror on the sun visor above the passenger seat and reapplied her lipstick. Too many Chicken McNuggets had undermined her cosmetic work.

She smeared on the ruby-red, pressed her lips together, and frowned. She hated McDonald's. The only edible food in the whole restaurant was the french fries, and they weren't exactly conducive to a 114-pound hourglass figure.

Still, Frank had seemed to think it was important that they all trudge out to the dreadful place, not that he'd bothered to explain why. She thought it was strange. But not as strange as this business of stopping at a church — First Presbyterian, just off Robinson. As far as she knew, Frank never went near churches, and for a reason. But today, when probably half the congregation was crowding in for the

Christmas Eve service, he did.

But even that was not as strange as what happened next. Frank returned from his brief sojourn inside the holy halls — wearing a Santa suit.

"I know the man who plays Santa here," Frank whispered to Bonnie when he returned to the car. "He's a good guy. And he knows how to keep his mouth shut."

Bonnie shook her head in quiet amazement. Curiouser and curiouser.

Frank shut the door behind him, then twisted around to face Tommy, who was slumped down in the backseat. "Hey, Tommy. Tell Santa whether you've been a good boy this year."

Tommy barely raised his eyes. "You're not Santa."

"But of course I am. Don't you see this beard?" He pulled it down by its elastic string and popped it back against his chin. "Ho, ho, ho."

Tommy averted his eyes and made a nasty face.

"Now, son —"

"I'm not your son!"

Frank lowered his chin. "Tommy, you have to answer Santa's question. Naughty or nice?"

"Leave me alone."

Frank made a *tsk*ing sound. "Naughty. Definitely naughty."

They drove the rest of the way home in silence. Bonnie still didn't know what was going on, so she decided to stop worrying about it. She tilted her seat back, relaxed, and waited to see what Santa would do next.

When they arrived at Bonnie's house, Frank parked the car in the driveway. Tommy cracked open his car door.

"Not yet," Frank instructed him.

Tommy frowned. "What are we waiting for?"

"You're waiting till I say you're not waiting." Frank checked his watch.

A few minutes later, when the watch read almost nine-thirty, he spoke again. "All right then. Let's get out now."

Tommy sprang out of the backseat. He had almost reached the front door of the house when he heard Frank calling him.

"Tommy? I have something for you."

"What?"

"This." The instant Tommy turned around, Frank smacked him hard across the face.

Tommy staggered backward. He lost his balance and fell in a heap onto the concrete steps below the front porch.

181

Bonnie was utterly bewildered. "Have lost your mind, Frank?"

He looked pointedly at her. "Carl," he said. "Have you lost your mind, *Carl*."

Bonnie stared at her Santa-suited boyfriend, and suddenly, she understood. All the pieces fell into place. "Carl," she murmured, and then she turned the volume up. "Have you lost your mind, Carl?" she shouted.

"Yeah," Frank muttered. "I'm out of control." He reached down and hit Tommy again, this time clubbing him on the other side of his face.

Tommy screamed, but Bonnie screamed even louder. "Help! Someone help! He's hurting my baby!"

Lightbulbs flickered on the porches of some of the neighboring houses.

"You ain't seen nothin' yet," Frank said. He raised Tommy up by the collar, then punched him in the soft part of the stomach.

Tommy hurt so badly he couldn't speak. He doubled over and fell to the grass.

"You miserable brat," Frank bellowed. "I'll beat you till you can't see straight." He reared back a foot and kicked Tommy in the side.

"No!" Bonnie glanced over her shoulder.

She could see silhouetted figures standing in the windows of other houses. The audience was assembling. "I can't control him, Tommy! Run! Run!"

Tommy staggered to his feet and limped toward the house. Frank made a show of starting after him, and Bonnie made a show of trying to restrain him. "No, Carl. I won't let you hurt my boy!"

"You can't stop me," Frank cried. "I'm gonna kill him!"

Even Bonnie was startled. Frank's performance was becoming altogether too convincing. "No!" she shouted. "Stop!"

"I'll teach that boy a lesson he won't soon forget!" Frank shouted. He pushed Bonnie away, then raced into the house.

A moment later, Bonnie followed. She knew the neighbors were watching, knew that someone was undoubtedly calling the police. Everything was in place now.

Perfect.

Megan's hands gripped the steering wheel. It seemed as if she had spent the entire day this way — racing through parking lots, careening through intersections, blitzing down I-35 at speeds way beyond what her little Toyota was used to handling. Now, for the second time today, she was racing to her new client's home in Kensington Park. Only this time she had the dire feeling that if she didn't get there soon, someone was going to end up dead.

She zoomed off the interstate and headed crosstown, by the fairgrounds. There was so much happening, she couldn't possibly make sense of it. All she knew for sure was this — Carl Cantrell was not what he had been made out to be. He was being set up.

And why? Megan could only think of one possible explanation. And it sent chills down her spine.

The radio was on, playing some insipid Christmas song, dogs barking to the tune of "Jingle Bells." She spun the dial, hoping to catch some evening news. On the third station she tried, she found what she wanted:

". . . that the explosion was minor. Although a great deal of smoke and noise resulted, there was little actual property damage. Still, in the confusion, suspect Carl Cantrell managed to escape his police escort and is now running free. I repeat, at seven-thirty this evening, at St. Anthony's Hospital, an explosion resulted from . . . ."

Seven-thirty, Megan thought bitterly, glancing at the clock on her dashboard.

And now it was almost nine-thirty. More than enough time for Carl to find his way back to Bonnie's house. To see his son on Christmas Eve. There was not the slightest doubt in her mind — she knew that was what he would do.

An aching in her chest reminded her what was likely to happen the instant he showed up.

Too late, Megan saw the exit for the Kensington development. She crossed three lines of traffic, making an almost diagonal line across the highway. She heard the screeching brakes of cars in the other lanes as she sped in front of them. If she rolled down her window, she could probably hear a few choice remarks flung in her direction, too. She couldn't think about that now, couldn't worry about it. She knew she was driving recklessly, but she had no choice. She had to get to that house.

She careened down the exit ramp and screeched to a halt. Swerving left hard, she headed toward the Kensington. She barreled down the road, full speed ahead. She had to get there in time, she *had* to, no matter how impossible it seemed. Blast! If ever there was a time when she could use a little faith, this was it.

She glanced up at the sky, but she didn't hear any voices speaking to her. The only voice she heard was the ballistics expert:

No doubt about it. That bullet came from inside the house.

And if a bullet came from that house once, Megan had no doubt that it could do so again.

Carl leaped over the fence, swinging himself by his hands. His agility was considerably hampered by the oversized black plastic boots he was wearing, not to mention the thick stuffing sewed into the suit. It might be important that Santa be a right jolly old elf during shopping mall appearances, but tonight, it was just a pain in the butt. He lost his balance, tipped sideways, and fell onto the wet grass.

It had been snowing for at least half an hour now, while he ran all the way crosstown to get here. And the truth was, Santa's suit wasn't nearly as warm as it looked. What's worse, the pain medication was wearing off, and his arm was beginning to remind him that he had been shot today.

But he had to put all that out of his mind. Tommy needed him. Tommy was in deadly danger. He had to save Tommy.

He had no problem with coming through the back; he didn't want to be stopped by any busybody neighbors either. After punching a few of them and creating major scenes in the front yard, he knew it wouldn't take much to get their attention. At the very least they would call the cops, and Carl couldn't let that happen. The cops would only haul him away. They'd leave Tommy in the clutches of Frank, and maybe his mother — whoever it was that was hurting him. No, it was important that Carl be able to get in, get Tommy, and get away.

He ran up to the sliding door in the back of the house. Sure enough, it was unlocked. He pushed it open and slipped inside.

Everything was quiet. Where were the sounds of misery he had heard over the phone? Or alternatively, the sounds of Christmas Eve revelry?

He raced upstairs to check for signs of life. Tommy's room was empty. It was a mess, books and toys scattered all over, his Star Wars pajamas lying in a heap on the floor. But no Tommy.

He checked the other rooms as well. No Frank, no Bonnie. He couldn't understand it. What was going on here?

Had they gone somewhere for Christmas Eve? Carl knew Bonnie didn't have any relatives in the area. Maybe Frank? Maybe out to dinner? A million possibilities ran through his head, some of them positive, and some of them . . .

His imagination conjured hideous dark notions. What if Bonnie decided to do what he'd planned to do? What if she'd taken Tommy away, who knows where, to start over again without her ex-husband screwing everything up for her? What if they'd hurt Tommy, maybe bad, and taken him away to hide what they'd done? Taken him away — or taken the body . . .

Carl's fists balled up with rage. Tommy was his boy; he was supposed to protect him. And he'd failed. He'd failed in the most desperate, pitiful, fatal —

He started abruptly. He'd heard something — some kind of a noise. But it wasn't coming from inside the house. It was coming from the front yard.

He peeked through the bedroom window. He could see Tommy and Bonnie and . . . and someone else in a Santa suit!

"You miserable brat," the other Santa shouted at the top of his lungs. "I'll beat you till you can't see straight!"

What was going on? Was that Frank? It

sounded like him. But why was he dressed in the suit?

The same suit Carl himself was wearing.

He didn't have time to ponder these questions. He heard the front door open, then slam shut. He ran down the stairs as quickly as possible to see who had come in.

"Tommy!" he shouted from midway down the stairs.

Tommy looked up. He was clutching his side; his face was contorted with pain. As soon as he saw the Santa suit on the stairs, he panicked.

"It's me," Carl said, pulling down the fake white beard so the boy could see. "It's me!"

"Daddy!" Tommy ran toward him, meeting him at the foot of the stairs. He threw his arms around his father, hugging him like he'd never hugged him before.

"Daddy," he said again, but more quietly this time. All at once his face was covered with tears, as if he'd been holding them back bravely as long as possible but just couldn't manage it any more. "I knew you'd come, Daddy," he whispered. "I knew you'd save me."

Carl hugged his son back, squeezing with all his might. He'd dreamed of this moment. He'd been desperate for it for years. And now that it was finally here, he wouldn't let anything interfere —

"Well, now, isn't this a scene out of Currier and Ives?"

Carl whirled around, without releasing his son.

Frank stood in the entryway, still looking like Carl's mirror image in red fur and fake whiskers. Bonnie was just a step behind him, closing the door.

"What the hell's going on here?" Carl asked.

Frank was the picture of nonchalance. He sashayed past Carl, barely even glancing at him. "Whatever are you talking about?"

"I'm talking about you hitting my boy!"

Frank flopped down onto the white plush sofa. "But that wasn't me, Carl. That was you."

"Are you crazy? I wouldn't hit my own son."

"Ah, but that's not what the neighbors will say. Or anyone else, for that matter."

"What are you talking about? I was very careful — no one saw me come in."

"Oh, but you're wrong, Carl." He flipped a cigarette out of his pocket and lit it. "Everyone saw you come in. Everyone saw you flip out of control, like a drunken madman. Everyone saw you beating your son within an inch of his life." He glanced pointedly at Bonnie. "I wouldn't be surprised if the poor lad died from it."

"I don't know what you're babbling about, Frank." Carl eased toward the front door, taking Tommy with him. "I'm leaving now and Tommy's going with me. And you're not going to stop me."

"It's true," Frank said wearily. Another pointed glance at Bonnie. "*I'm* not going to stop you."

Carl didn't know what was going on, but he also knew it would be stupid to stand around trying to figure it out. The smartest thing he could do was make a run for it while he had the chance.

"C'mon, Tommy," he said. He broke the boy's embrace but scooped up his hand. "We're leaving."

Son in tow, he ran to the front door, threw it open, and ran into the front yard. "Do you feel well enough to run?" he asked Tommy.

Tommy's head bobbed up and down, but Carl could tell his heart wasn't in it. They would have to move slowly. Still, they should be able to get away. As long as there wasn't any interference . . .

"Stop!"

Carl knew he shouldn't stop, shouldn't even look, but he couldn't help himself. He turned.

Bonnie was standing on the front porch. In the few seconds he had been conversing with Frank, she had totally altered her appearance. Her clothes were torn; her dress was hanging from one shoulder strap and was ripped open in the front. Her makeup was smeared; her hair was a mess. Her face looked wet and bruised.

As if someone had just attacked her. Attacked and beat her.

There was one other alteration in her appearance, one Carl noticed almost immediately.

She was now holding a small handgun. And it was pointed toward his head.

22

"I'm not letting you take Tommy!" Bonnie shouted. Her voice was abnormally loud, and Carl realized it wasn't for his benefit. She was playing for the larger audience.

"Bonnie," he whispered. "Don't do this."

"I won't let you hurt him!" she continued, still shouting. "I won't let you beat him like you did me. Like you've beat him so many times before!"

"Bonnie, please." He pulled Tommy close to him. "I'm begging you."

"You've made us live like slaves, like prisoners. Always in fear of when you might strike again." It was like she was shouting lines from a play, lines she had practiced and rehearsed in the mirror well ahead of time. "I know if you beat Tommy again, you'll kill him. I'm his mother, Carl. I can't let that happen."

Carl couldn't think what to do. He felt paralyzed, frozen. If he tried to run, she might shoot him. But if he stayed still, she almost certainly would.

"Don't try to run off with Tommy," she said. "I won't let you take him. I won't let you hide him away somewhere and kill him slowly."

That was it, Carl realized. It was like a cue. She wanted him to run, so she'd have an excuse for shooting him. Well, he wouldn't give it to her. If she was going to shoot him, it was going to have to be in cold blood. With a stationary target.

"I just hope you haven't killed Tommy already," she continued, still blasting out each word. "He's hurt so bad."

Carl squeezed Tommy closer to him. "Bonnie — *no!*"

Bonnie held the gun out at the farthest extreme with both hands. "I'm sorry it has to be this way, Carl. But I can't let this go on. I won't let you kill me. I won't let you kill Tommy."

It was coming now. Carl could feel it. He could sense that the dialogue had ended and the time had come for action.

He looked down at his son. "I love you, Tommy," he whispered. "I always have. Always will."

"Carl, no!" Bonnie shouted for the benefit of the invisible audience. "I won't let you hurt him! I won't let you!"

He could see her hands tightening, see the tiny bones in her hand flexing around the trigger. It seemed she'd reached the end of the script.

He closed his eyes and waited for the end to come.

Megan surveyed the tableau in the space of a heartbeat. She might not understand all the details, but she certainly comprehended the main event. Bonnie was pointing a gun at Carl, tensing up to shoot.

Megan didn't stop to ask questions. She flung herself against Bonnie, tackling her like a tight end sacking a quarterback. They both crashed to the ground, but Bonnie was on the bottom and she took the worst of it. Megan heard a loud exhalation in her ear and knew that she'd at least knocked the wind out of the woman.

Unfortunately, Bonnie was down but not out. She reached up with her gun hand and clubbed Megan on the top of her head. The hard metal dug into her scalp, cutting a jagged dent in the left side. Megan could feel blood rising to the surface.

Megan gritted her teeth and pushed Bonnie's arm away. Her brain was racing.

What should she do next? Somehow, hand-to-hand combat had never been covered back at seminary. She had to try whatever first came to mind, whatever was available.

Bonnie's head was just beyond Megan's knees. She grabbed Bonnie's head and slammed it back against the ground.

That seemed to take the woman for a loop. Her eyes rolled back and the lids fluttered.

Megan moved fast while she had some slight advantage. She lifted one leg back and drove her knee into the woman's solar plexus.

Bonnie let out an "oof!" and all at once the fight went out of her body. Unfortunately, she was still holding the gun. Megan crawled across Bonnie's body and clamped down on her arm, just below the wrist. She raised it up and down, pounding it against the hard wet grass. After several poundings, the gun spilled out of her hand.

Carl rushed forward, kicking the gun away. "Thank God you arrived. Another second and she would've —"

"Yeah, I saw." Megan rolled Bonnie over and pinned her arms behind her back. She was beginning to stir; Megan wanted to make sure she was in no condition to struggle. "Lucky timing."

"Lucky?" Carl shook his head. "More like a miracle."

Miracle? Megan looked up at him, but at that moment, she heard the sirens of police cars wailing up the residential street. "Let me talk to them," Megan said. "I don't understand this mess perfectly, but I probably understand it better than you."

"No contest."

Megan glanced down at the bundle of flesh she was sitting on. "Make sure your ex-wife doesn't go anywhere, okay?"

Carl grabbed Bonnie's wrists. "It'll be a pleasure."

After what seemed like an eternity, Megan returned to Carl. The police had taken Bonnie out of his custody; he was sitting on the front porch steps now, waiting to hear what lay in his future. If he had a future.

"Well, I think I got that straightened out for the time being, anyway," Megan said. She sat beside him on the porch step.

"You mean they believed you?"

Megan nodded. "I made them call their ballistics expert." She gestured toward the police officers, now returning to their cars with Bonnie. "And the coroner — the man who examined your arm wound. Both of them had evidence that backed up my story and made the police realize what Bonnie and Frank were doing."

"Then I'm off the hook?"

"Well, let's not go overboard. There's still the matter of the neighbor you injured. The housebreaking. The escape from custody. But there are also some keenly mitigating circumstances. It'll be a while before the cops have finished their investigation. I promised you wouldn't leave town."

"Sure, no problem."

"But the most important thing is — you won't be spending Christmas behind bars."

Carl's lips parted, but he didn't speak. His eyes became wide and watery.

"Which is good, because Tommy isn't going to have anyone else to stay with."

There was a catch in Carl's throat. "You mean, I'm going to spend Christmas with —" He suddenly let out a gasp. "Look out!"

Megan whirled around to see a man she knew must be Frank flying toward her, fists first. She screamed.

Carl grabbed her by the arm and yanked her out of Frank's path, barely a second before he landed. Where had he come from? Megan puzzled. In the space of a heartbeat, she realized he must've hidden in a back bedroom, then dropped out of a window as soon as the police left the house.

"You've ruined everything," Frank growled. His eyes were blazing; the expression on his face said he could kill anyone and anything that came into his grasp. Then he lunged.

Carl shoved Megan out of the way. Frank hit Carl front and center, knocking him down onto the porch — hard. A moment later, Frank scrabbled to his feet and took off.

Carl pushed himself up from the pavement slowly. Blood was trickling from the side of his mouth.

Megan laid a restraining hand on his shoulder. "Let the police catch him."

"Like hell." Carl started after Frank. Megan followed. She realized she must be seeing Carl's police training in action. It rose to the surface even when Carl wasn't consciously thinking about it. He was fast, too. In no time at all, he'd left her far behind.

Carl caught Frank just before he crossed the neighbor's yard. He wrapped himself around Frank's legs, knocking him to the ground. Before the man could recover, he rolled Frank onto his back and sat on him, pinning his arms back.

"Go ahead," Carl said. "Resist. Please."

Frank's teeth were clenched; his face was smeared with dirt and grass stains. He drank in the cold hard look in Carl's eyes — and did not resist.

A phone call later, two police officers came running to the scene. "Nice work," one of them said to Carl as he snapped the cuffs around Frank's wrists. "Thanks for the assist."

"Any time."

Carl pushed off Frank's prostrate body, then walked over to Megan. "Well, that was fun. Maybe I'm not totally washed up after all."

Megan smiled. "I'm certain of it."

"Did you mean what you said before? About me spending Christmas with —" All at once, his face darkened. "Tommy!"

"What about him?"

Carl slapped himself on the side of the head. "I'm such an idiot. In all the confusion, I lost track of him. He was so terrified when his mother was pointing that gun at us. Then he ran inside and —" His eyes darted to one side, and then his voice disappeared.

Megan laid her hand on his shoulder. "Carl? What is it?"

His hand rose, trembling, and pointed to the place on the grass where Bonnie had been tackled. "The gun," he said, barely getting the word out. "I kicked it over by the hedge."

"Yeah. So?"

"It's gone." He turned to face Megan, his eyes wide with fear. "And so is Tommy."

23

Megan tiptoed carefully up the stairs of the house. Tommy's room was at the top and the door was closed.

She stepped carefully toward his door. She stood to one side and knocked gently. "Tommy?"

"Don't come in!" he shouted from inside. The words seemed to pour out of him, like water from a fountain. "I've got a gun! I'll shoot!"

Well, that solved that mystery. Tommy had the gun. And he was holed up in his room, thinking heaven only knew what, trying to keep the monsters at bay.

"Tommy, listen to me. I'm your friend."

"You're my mother's friend!" the boy shouted through the door. "You helped her take me away from my dad!"

She pressed her hand against her forehead. This was going to be harder than she imagined. Carl was searching downstairs;

she thought about getting him, making him do this. But the truth was, whoever turned that doorknob was putting his or her life in danger. And more than anything else, Tommy needed to have a father, alive, not in the hospital and not in jail, when Christmas Day rolled around.

She touched the doorknob. "Tommy, I'm just going to step inside. And you're not going to fire that pistol."

"I will!" There was a desperate urgency in his voice, a pronounced note of panic. She didn't doubt for a minute that he was capable of pulling that trigger. "I'll shoot anyone who comes through the door!"

"Tommy, listen to me. There's no reason to be angry. I know there are people who've hurt you. But the police have taken the bad people away."

"I'm tellin' you — don't open that door!" Tommy's voice trembled as he spoke. "If you do, I'll shoot!"

Megan felt for the boy so strongly her heart ached. He was frightened to death. And who could blame him? He was only seven years old, after all. He'd seen his father acting like a crazy man, his mother pointing a gun at him, her boyfriend beating him within an inch of his life. Who wouldn't be scared? And confused. And ready to do anything to prevent it from starting all over again.

"Tommy, listen to me."

"I won't! I'll shoot! Don't think I don't know how to fire this gun. I do!"

Megan crouched down on the floor and peered through the crack between the door and the jamb. It was just wide enough for her to see a tiny sliver of the room inside.

She gasped, then pressed her hand against her throat. Tommy was holding the gun backwards, so the barrel pointed at himself. If he pulled the trigger, he'd blow a hole in his chest the size of a canyon.

"Tommy, listen to me! You can't fire that gun. You might hurt yourself. Or even —"

"I will! I'll fire if you turn that doorknob!"

"Tommy, *no!*" Megan could feel her own panic rising. She had to beat it down, keep her wits about her. "Tommy, please listen to what I have to say. There's no reason to be scared. Frank is in custody and he'll never be able to lay a hand on you again. You're absolutely safe. I'm a lawyer, Tommy. Trust me. The law will protect you."

"That's what they all say!" Tommy replied. He was screaming now; he sounded as if he was about to lose control altogether. "I won't believe you. *I won't!*"

Megan took a deep breath and slowly released it. Her palms were sweating, but somehow, she had to remain calm. If she was going to talk him out of this, it clearly wasn't going to be as a lawyer. There had to be another way.

"Tommy, please relax. I'm not coming in. I'm not even near the door." She waited for a moment, didn't hear anything. With any luck, he was calming a bit. "Tommy, I'm not just a lawyer. I'm also a priest. Do you know what a priest is?"

There was a long pause before he answered. "Like — sort of a preacher?"

"That's exactly right, Tommy. Now listen to me — you know what day today is, don't you?"

" 'Course I do. I'm not stupid. It's Christmas Eve."

"That's exactly right." Megan glanced at her watch. Only a few minutes till the big day itself. "Now, Tommy, do you know what Christmas is? Do you know why we celebrate this day?"

"I know what they say. S'posed to be when Jesus was born. 'Cept it prob'ly isn't."

"Well, you're right, Tommy. It probably isn't. But that's not the point. The point is

that we have a special day when we remember who Jesus is. What he did." She
paused, then crept a bit closer to the door.
"Have you heard any stories about Jesus?"

His voice was totally noncommittal.
"Yeah. Some."

"Well, then, you've probably heard the
stories about when Jesus was a baby. He
had a tough Christmas Eve, too, you know.
His parents had to go on a big trip. No one
would give them a place to stay. He was
born in a barn and had to sleep in a pig
trough." She paused. "I bet he was scared,
too."

Tommy's voice seemed quieter. "Yeah.
Maybe so."

"But he didn't let it get to him, Tommy.
He tried to be brave about it. And when he
grew up, he did many wonderful things."
She didn't know where she was going with
this. She was babbling like some insipid
Sunday-school teacher, trying unsuccessfully to make a point. A point she couldn't
really make — because she didn't believe it
herself.

She heard a clock chiming somewhere
downstairs. It was midnight. Christmas
Day had arrived.

Almost without thinking about it, she
turned her eyes upward. All right, God, if

you're really up there, if you want me to have faith, give me something to have faith in. You wouldn't save the 169 people in the Murrah building, and you wouldn't save my mommy. Would you at least *please* save this little boy?

She laid her head gently against the door. She was so tired. But she knew she couldn't stop, not now. "Tommy," she said, barely above a whisper, "if you fire that gun, you could ruin the entire rest of your life. You could hurt me" — she paused — "you could even hurt yourself. Please don't do that, Tommy. Remember, Jesus was scared sometimes too, but he never hurt anyone, and he always tried to do the right thing." She pressed herself against the closed door. She didn't know what else she could do, what else she could say. "I know you want to do the right thing, Tommy. I know you do. So please, *please* put down that gun."

She heard a soft thump on the carpet. She could see through the crack that he had dropped the gun, but she also knew he could pick it up again just as quickly. There was no way she could be sure —

She was just going to have to have faith.

She turned the doorknob and stepped inside.

Tommy was crouched in the corner of his room, nestled behind his bed. His face was streaked with tears. The gun lay on the floor just before him.

Megan ran into the room. She kicked the gun far away, then cradled him in her arms.

"Thank you, Tommy," she said softly, and she suddenly realized tears were springing from her own eyes as well. She squeezed him impossibly tightly. "Thank you for trusting me." Her eyes turned toward the ceiling. "And thank you, too," she whispered. "Thanks for being here when I really needed you."

Carl appeared in the doorway. "Did you . . ." His eyes scanned the room, saw the gun on the other side of the floor. "Is anybody . . . ?"

"No," Megan said. She laughed, then realized she was crying and laughing, both at once. "We're all fine."

"Thank God." Carl picked up the gun and carefully removed all the bullets. "Another miracle."

Megan smiled, then squeezed Tommy all the tighter. "What did you expect?" she said, beaming. "It's Christmas."

24

It had taken some doing, but Megan had finally managed to persuade Carl and Tommy to spend Christmas Day at her house. It was a perfect arrangement. Carl readily admitted that his broken-down apartment was not the most festive location for a father-son reunion. Megan, on the other hand, had a tree, mistletoe, and all the best Christmas videos. And none of them wanted to be alone.

Carl and Megan sat on the sofa, sipping some hot cider Megan had whipped up. The snow had blanketed her house; not a huge snow, but two or three inches seemed like a lot in Oklahoma City in December. Tommy sat at their feet, near the television, watching *How the Grinch Stole Christmas* for the second time through.

Jasper released a burst of concentrated gas, reminding all present, and possibly some of the neighbors, of his presence.

Looking rather sheepish, he hobbled up to Megan and nuzzled his head in her lap, leaving a dark puddle of drool all over her Christmas sweatshirt.

"You know," Megan said to Carl, "a boy Tommy's age ought to have a dog . . ."

"Forget it," Carl said firmly. "Not a chance."

"Well, it was worth a try." She went to the kitchen and poured some Alpo into Jasper's bowl, momentarily distracting him. After the coast was clear, she returned to the sofa.

"I think he's going to be all right," Carl said quietly, without explaining. He didn't need to. Megan knew perfectly well what he was talking about. She had been just as worried about Tommy, how he would deal with the trauma of the past day, the past years. But all the early signs were indicating that he was well on the road to healing. She knew there would be tough times ahead for Carl and his son, but she also had a strong sense that they would be able to ride it through.

"He's a tough kid," Carl added. "And very smart. I think he understands more than we realize. Probably has all along."

"I know he's happy to be with his daddy again," Megan said. "I think he feels safe — maybe for the first time he can remember."

Carl nodded. "He's a good boy." He jabbed Megan playfully in the side. "You're not so bad yourself."

"Aw shucks."

"You've made this a wonderful day for us. Thank you."

Megan smiled. "It has been a wonderful day. I just wish my mother —" She turned away, shook her head. "I'm sorry. Never mind."

Carl stretched out his legs. "Tell you what. I've got a proposition for you."

Megan arched an eyebrow. "Should we ask Tommy to leave the room?"

"Nothing like that. I was thinking — why don't you and I set up shop together?"

"I beg your pardon?"

"You heard me. Let's start our own business."

"I see. One of those lawyer/ex-cop shops."

"You need to get out of that law firm. You hate it and you know it. It's killing you, or at least your spirit. You need to set up your own office."

"With you?"

"Well, I figure you can't do everything yourself. You're going to need someone to handle all the administrative tasks. Run errands. Do the gofering. And at some point, once you start building up a caseload, you may even need an investigator. Having an ex-cop around might not be such a bad idea."

Megan shook her head. "Do you have any idea how much it costs to set up your own firm?"

"No, but what does it matter? As luck would have it, your gofer is fabulously wealthy."

"I thought you didn't get any of it until —"

"That's just around the corner, relatively speaking. In the meantime, I'll borrow against what I'm going to get in the future. It'll work, believe me."

Megan bit down on her lower lip. It was tempting, she had to admit. The chance to get out of the firm, to stop wasting her energy on corporate bigwigs and start helping those who really need help. But it was so uncertain . . .

"You know, Carl, it would be incredibly risky. Most small businesses crash and burn in the first year."

"I know it will be tough. But we can do it. I know we can. If we could get through yesterday, we can get through anything."

Megan stared deeply into his eyes. She

wanted to believe him. She wanted to believe in miracles. But it was so hard . . .

"I want to turn my life around," Carl said quietly. "I want to be a good daddy. I want to do good work." He reached out abruptly and touched Megan's hand. "But I don't want to do it alone."

His words sent a chill down her spine. There was that word again: *alone*. The same word that had haunted her yesterday, and haunted Carl too, it seemed. No one wanted to be alone. Especially not at Christmas.

"I don't mean to be rude, Carl, but I think you still have some issues to work through. I think you need serious counseling."

"I'll do whatever you want me to do."

"You'll have to give up the booze. And I mean, totally. Not a drop."

He lowered his eyes. "I'll — I'll do my best. I've been going to meetings and —"

She nodded. "And now you won't be doing it by yourself. I know some counselors who are fabulous. A carryover from my priestly days. And of course" — she averted her eyes — "I'll be around. Anytime you need a little help."

"Thank you, Megan. So about my proposition?"

"Well," she said, smiling, "in for a penny, in for a pound. Let's do it."

He squeezed her hand tightly. "You won't regret this."

The Grinch returned the toys to the citizens of Whoville, and soon the end credits were scrolling. Tommy was beginning to look restless.

"I just wish I had a present for him," Carl whispered. "I went to the toy store yesterday and tried to buy something, but it was a total mob scene."

"That's a shame," Megan said. "Every little boy ought to have something —" She snapped her fingers. "Wait a minute. I have a present for him!"

"You do?"

"Yes. From the man in ballistics. He was going to give it to his little boy, but he wasn't going to see him at Christmas and —"

"So he gave it to you?"

"Well, I gave him this little plastic bus."

"Excuse me?"

"It all started with a tacky black-velvet picture of bulldogs playing five-card stud —"

"I'm afraid you've lost me."

She shook her hands in the air. "Never mind. It's a long story." She jumped up and ran out to her car to get the present. While Tommy was distracted, she slipped the wrapped bundle into Carl's hands. "I think it should come from you," she whispered.

"But what is it?"

"Beats me. But any present is better than none, right?"

"I suppose." He leaned forward. "Hey, Tommy. You haven't opened your present yet."

Tommy's head whipped around the instant the word *present* was spoken. "For me?"

"Yes, of course for you. It's Christmas, remember?" He tossed the gift to Tommy.

Tommy didn't wait a second. He ripped off the wrapping paper and tore open the box.

"Dad!" Tommy cried. "You found it!"

Carl blinked. "I did?"

Tommy ran forward and threw his arms around his father. "You found it!" He squeezed Carl with all his might, then planted a kiss on his cheek. "Thank you, Daddy."

Carl resisted the urge to shrug. "My pleasure."

"What is it?" Megan asked.

Tommy was so full of excitement he

could barely speak. "It's the Mighty Movin' Dino-Fighter. With the Power Pack!"

Carl's jaw dropped. "It is?"

Megan looked from father to son. "Is that good?"

"It's exactly what I wanted!" Tommy cried. "But how did you get it, Dad? When we went to Toys "Я" Us, they didn't have any."

Carl glanced over at Megan, then looked wordlessly back at his son. "It's Christmas, son. That's the season of miracles."

"Wow. Can I play with it now?"

"I don't see why not."

Tommy ran back to the center of the room and began assembling all the plastic parts. Carl leaned close to Megan's ear. "What do you suppose are the odds . . ."

"I don't even want to think about it," she said firmly.

Tommy plunged headfirst into animated play with his new acquisition, and Megan and Carl resettled on the sofa.

"I just can't get over . . . how wonderful all this is," Carl said, his voice choking. "I was so certain I would be spending Christmas alone. And now . . ." He shook his head in amazement. "I just wish I had something for you. You've done so much for us."

"Don't worry about it," Megan answered. "You'll have plenty of time to make up for it. Like when you start bankrolling my new law firm."

"Yeah, but in the meantime. I'd like to do something."

"Fine. In another hour, Jasper's going to need his suppository."

Carl laughed. "You know what I mean. Like a present. Today is Christmas, after all."

She looked away. "Don't be silly. I'm a grown-up. I don't need Christmas presents."

"If you say so." His eyes narrowed a bit. "Then what's that present under the tree?"

"Present? What?"

"See? Way in the back." He pointed it out for her.

Megan crossed the room and crawled behind the tree. "I can't imagine who —" She picked up the hatbox-sized wrapped package and lifted the flap on the card.

TO MY MEGAN, it read. FROM YOUR MOMMY.

"Mother?" She felt as if the air had suddenly been sucked out of her lungs. "But —"

She didn't wait to figure it all out. Moving faster than Tommy had opening the Mighty Movin' Dino-Fighter, she ripped off the wrapping paper.

The cardboard box inside was sealed with a strip of packaging tape. She pressed her fingernail into the crease and dragged it across the box.

One flap popped free. Megan pulled open the other.

And examined the contents.

It was a Kewpie doll, just like the dozen in her office, just like all the others her mother had given her every time she was going somewhere. But this one was different. This one was wearing a long white gown. She was holding a harp and had wings sprouting out of her back.

And there was a halo over her head.

Megan fished around inside the box till she found the card:

Thanks so much for letting me go. I'm happy now. And I want you to be happy, too. I will always always love you. Mom.

Megan placed the package on the coffee table and fell into the nearest chair. Tears cascaded down her face.

Carl leaned forward, concerned. "Is something wrong?"

"No," Megan said, biting down on her lip. "Something is right. Very, very right."

"I — don't understand."

"Doesn't matter." She shook her head, and her voice trembled as she spoke. "I — I just realized how wrong I've been. About so many things." She wiped the teardrops from her eyes. "But the biggest mistake was when I thought I was alone. I'm not alone. I was never alone."

She took his hand and they both sat silently for a long stretch, each quietly contemplating what a ceramic Kewpie doll and a Mighty Movin' Dino-Fighter could tell them about the season of miracles.

About the Author

William Bernhardt made his debut as a novelist with *Primary Justice*. His subsequent novels include *Blind Justice, Deadly Justice, Perfect Justice* — which won the Oklahoma Book Award and led *The Vancouver Sun* to dub the author "the American equivalent of P. G. Wodehouse or John Mortimer" — *Double Jeopardy, Cruel Justice, Naked Justice, Extreme Justice*, and *Dark Justice*. As an attorney, Bernhardt has received several awards for his public service, and in 1993 he was named one of the top twenty-five young lawyers in the nation. He lives in Tulsa with his wife, Kirsten, and their children, Harry and Alice.

The employees of Thorndike Press hope you have enjoyed this Large Print book. All our Thorndike and Wheeler Large Print titles are designed for easy reading, and all our books are made to last. Other Thorndike Press Large Print books are available at your library, through selected bookstores, or directly from us.

For information about titles, please call:

(800) 223-1244

or visit our Web site at:

www.gale.com/thorndike
www.gale.com/wheeler

To share your comments, please write:

Publisher
Thorndike Press
295 Kennedy Memorial Drive
Waterville, ME   04901

35267